NOV 0 5 2007.

D0629622

VENICE PUBLIC LIBRARY
300 S. NOKOMIS AVENUE
VENICE, FL 34285

GOD OF LUCK

Also by the Author

FICTION

The Moon Pearl

Thousand Pieces of Gold

Wooden Fish Songs

NONFICTION

Sole Survivor

Chinese American Portraits: Personal Histories 1828–1988

JUVENILE

Pie-Biter

GOD OF LUCK

RUTHANNE LUM McCUNN

VENICE PUBLIC LIBRARY
300 S. NOKOMIS AVENUE
VENICE, FL 34285

3 1969 01835 3283

Copyright © 2007 by Ruthanne Lum McCunn

Published by Soho Press, Inc.
853 Broadway
New York, NY 10003

All rights reserved.

Library of Congress Cataloging in Publication Data

McCunn, Ruthanne Lum.
God of luck / Ruthanne Lum McCunn.
p. cm.
ISBN-13: 978-1-56947-466-2
ISBN-10: 1-56947-466-4

1. Kidnapping—China—Fiction. 2. Chinese—Peru—History—19th
century—Fiction. 3. Forced labor—Peru—Fiction. 4. Agricultural
laborers—Peru—History—19th century—Fiction. 5. Guano—Peru—
Fiction. 6. Islands—Peru—Fiction. I. Title.

PS3613.C38665G63 2007
813'.54—dc22
2006051247

Designed by Pauline Neuwirth, Neuwirth & Associates, Inc.

10 9 8 7 6 5 4 3 2 1

In memory of
my parents
who, torn apart by forces beyond their control,
remained steadfast in their struggle to reunite.

Also for
Him Mark Lai and Philip Choy,
whose ground-breaking histories about Chinese America
continue to inspire me,
and who, with their wives,
Laura and Sarah,
have shown me unstinting generosity.

"The strong survive. The ones who are strong and *lucky*."
—JOHN EDGAR WIDEMAN, *Brothers and Keepers*

"The function of freedom is to free someone else."
—TONI MORRISON

From 1840 to 1875, multinational commercial interests operated a traffic in Asian labor to Latin America and the Caribbean. Of the estimated one million men decoyed or stolen from southern China, close to 100,000 landed in Peru.

GOD OF LUCK

PROLOGUE

A LONG-AGO emperor ordered dwarves enslaved for his amusement. The dwarves and their families wept. Fear swept through the kingdom that the bondage of little people would eventually lead to the servitude of all. Yet there were no protests. The emperor was too well known for his quick temper and cruel punishments.

Finally, one person found the courage to challenge the emperor in a petition: *No one, not even you, has the right to enslave another.*

The emperor bristled. The petitioner's bravery, however, moved him deeply, and instead of unleashing his temper, the emperor freed the dwarves and renounced slavery.

Everybody rejoiced at their good fortune, and they immortalized the petitioner as Fook Sing Gung, the God of Luck.

THE FIRST THREE or four years of my life, even family members sometimes mistook me for my twin sister. So when Old Lady Chow, our near neighbor in Strongworm Village, swooped me up, crowing, "Moongirl," I was not surprised.

"I'm Ah Lung."

"Really?" Pinning my knobby elbows and scrawny arms against her chest with one arm, Old Lady Chow jerked open the front of my split-bottomed pants with her free hand. "You're right! There *is* a dragon in here."

Her grip and rough handling belied her kindly tone, and I squirmed, flailed my legs, butted my head against her chest, struggling to break free.

"A very *little* dragon, mind. *So* little, it looks more worm than dragon to me. I know! You make it grow, and I'll believe you *are* Ah Lung."

I was, of course, too young to understand her meaning.

But a chick needs no explaining to know it's been snared by a hawk, and I sank my teeth into Old Lady Chow's forearm, forcing her to release me with an angry shriek.

TWENTY YEARS LATER, I was in the market town downriver where my brother and I had gone to sell our family's silk. Although younger than Fourth Brother, I was taller, broader in the shoulders, and well muscled. So I stood by the boat to guard our load of silk skeins while he took a sample into town to show buyers.

Suddenly, a stranger poked a sharp, long-nailed finger in my chest, demanding I repay him. This man was thin as a stick, his skin wizened as if he'd been fried in oil. But I was wearing the wide-brimmed bamboo hat, patched cotton jacket, and pants of a peasant; he wore the high-collared, side-slit robe and skullcap of gentry. I didn't dare catch hold of his slender wrists with my large-knuckled hands.

Moreover, I was keenly aware our family was never free of debt. It wasn't possible. Not with close to two dozen mouths to feed and greedy landowners squeezing us to fill their own coffers, to cover ever heavier taxes, the cost of building new dikes, the repair of old.

Ba only borrowed from the landlords in our village, however, and had I not been distracted by an acrobat tossing a stack of rice bowls into the air and catching them on top of his head, I'd have realized instantly we couldn't owe anything to a stranger and defended myself.

Before I could gather my wits, two hardfaced strongmen had seized me by my arms and legs. Storming through the knots of people crowding the riverbank, they shouted:

"This man owes money."

"We're taking him to the magistrate."

"Make way, make way."

At mention of the magistrate, people fell back. I squeezed both eyes shut and prayed Fourth Brother would return to our boat directly, discover what had happened to me from bystanders, and give chase. His tongue, quick as mine was slow, would at least give me a chance against my accuser's. Alone, I'd have none.

Abruptly, the strongmen threw me down. But there was no resounding boom from the magistrate's gong announcing the arrival of a petitioner. Instead, the ground under me gave way, jolting open my eyes: We were on the deck of a boat, a sampan not much larger than my family's skiff; my accuser's clothes were almost as faded and threadbare as my own.

Recognizing then that the charge of debt was a deliberate hoax, I thrust out my arms and legs. One fist brushed grizzled skin, a heel sank into soft flesh, another met bone. My abductors, bellowing their fury, threw themselves on top of me. The boat pitched crazily. Something hard smashed my skull, and I tumbled into stupefying nothingness.

THE SUFFOCATING DARKNESS was absolute. But I knew from the smooth rocking sensation, the steady slap-slap of water against wood, and the distinctive sound of a stern-oar grinding against a bearing pin that I was still on a boat. A boat small enough to require only the one oar. And since planking with a fishy stink was pressing against me from above and a chill damp was seeping through my cotton jacket and pants from below, I guessed that I was stuffed into the bottom of my abductors' sampan, that the moans and bony pressure on either side came from fellow captives.

Something rough bound my wrists and ankles, biting into my skin, numbing my hands and feet, my arms and legs. A splintery piece of wood between my teeth forced my tongue back into my throat. My stomach, rebelling, repeatedly seared my throat with bile. My lips and jaws, prized open so unnaturally, ached.

Desperate for air, I poked and prodded the board above with my nose, straining to find a crack. I twisted my head from side to side, grazing one ear, then the other against wood slick with slime in hopes of hearing something, anything, that would indicate help was on its way for me and the sharp-boned captives wedging me in.

How could I have been so careless? The waterpeddlers who traded in Strongworm brought news as well as goods, and as a small boy, I'd listened, slackjawed, to their tales of foreign devils whose greed knew no bounds. Not only did these devils carry off our men to labor for them in faraway lands, but they'd deliberately weakened our people with opium, then made war on us until nothing of our fleet— not a fragment of a sail or an oar—remained.

Thousands were thrown out of work or off their land during these wars. Which meant that their end did not bring an end to the fighting. Just that the fighting, whether it was clan against clan or peasants against gentry, was now between our own people—and the foreign devils were buying prisoners taken in these fights. They also employed pirates to kidnap unwary fishermen and raid coastal villages for men capable of heavy labor.

I hadn't been frightened. The clans in Strongworm and neighboring villages lived peaceably together, and we were far enough inland to be safe from pirates. After my twin, Moongirl, started working in Canton, however, she told us that men—city sophisticates as well as country bumpkins— were being stolen or decoyed, then sold as though they were pigs. And during her last visit home, Moongirl—her square face agitated, her voice weighted with concern—cautioned my brothers and me to be vigilant.

"Not only when you're on the river or in the market town, but here in Strongworm. The streets in the city have become so dangerous that if I were a man, I wouldn't dare step out of the house for fear of being kidnapped."

"Ai yah!" Second Brother, snaking his arm behind Third Brother, tweaked Moongirl's plait which hung down her back like a man's queue. "I know spinsters only comb up their hair on ceremonial occasions. But aren't you afraid you'll be mistaken for a man? Maybe you should join our wives in the kitchen instead of eating with us."

My brothers and I laughed. Moongirl, ignoring us, withdrew a paper from the inside pocket of her long, side-buttoned tunic, unfolded it. "Warnings have been posted all over."

Ba set down his bowl, held out a work-worn hand. "Let me see."

At his seriousness, our laughter faded. Moongirl rose, reached across the circular table, gave Ba the notice, and dropped back onto her stool. The clickety-click of chopsticks against bowls and dishes stopped. In the quiet, I realized there were no longer any sounds coming from the kitchen, where Ma was supervising Eldest and Fourth Sisters-in-law, or from the courtyard, where Second and Third Sisters-in-law were minding the children. Turning, I looked for my wife, Bo See.

She'd been serving. Now, motionless and beautiful as a jade carving, she was midway between the kitchen and the table in the common room where we were eating. Ma, her gaunt face more drawn than ever, hunched in the kitchen doorway. Behind her hovered plump Fourth Sister-in-law, lanky Eldest Sister-in-law; Second and Third Sisters-in-law, both similarly squat. Their eyes fixed on Ba, they were clearly waiting, as I was, for him to speak, to declare Moongirl's fears for us unfounded despite a deepening in the furrows of worry that creased his forehead, the ominous grinding of his teeth.

Third Brother tugged at his beetle brows. Second Brother's fleshy nostrils quivered. His eyesight too poor for him to read in the gray light of dusk, he made no attempt to peer over Ba's shoulder the way Eldest Brother was. Beside me, Fourth Brother cleared his throat ostentatiously, as if to prompt Ba or Eldest Brother.

When neither spoke, Fourth Brother suggested, "The city is surely too far away for us to be affected."

Ba's chest, clogged with catarrh, rumbled, and he stabbed a finger at the double column of characters on the paper. "There's a list of kidnapped men here that includes four from the Sun Duk district."

"Our district, yes," Eldest Brother acknowledged. "But they couldn't have been from any village near Strongworm *or* our market town or there'd have been talk. Lots of talk. And now that officials are offering rewards for the capture and prosecution of man-stealers, those rogues will go after other game."

Moongirl shook her head. "No sooner is one man-stealer caught and executed then another takes his place."

Astonished, I blurted, "Have they no fear?"

"No fear and no pity either," Moongirl said.

THAT MAN-STEALERS were without pity I did not doubt:
only people without a grain of human feeling would act
like beasts of prey. To beg my kidnappers for mercy, then,
would be a waste of spit.

But from what Moongirl and the waterpeddlers said,
the captains of the foreign devil-ships entered into agree-
ments with brokers for a set number of "piglets." These
brokers, in turn, negotiated with crimps in nearby dis-
tricts who sent out runners—like my kidnappers—to
bring in the number specified. And since money was what
these villains were after, why should they care whether it
came from a broker or my family?

Ba wouldn't have an extra copper to give them. But
Moongirl was making good money in the city, and she
would be willing to ransom me. Six years ago, she'd given
Ba the bride price for my wife, and my kidnappers'
demands would be less than Bo See's parents' had been.

According to Moongirl, brokers were getting a year's
wages for each man delivered. But a runner's share was no
more than a few dollars. I would offer my kidnappers double. No, triple, to ensure their acceptance and my return
to Bo See.

Just thinking about Bo See made my spirits rise. My
manhood, too. In truth, after six years together as man and
wife, I was as impatient for night and the privacy of our

sleeping room as I had been as a bridegroom. No, more. For Bo See and I had been strangers when we married, shy and uncertain. Now we were intimately familiar with each other's every curve and crevice, confident and joyful in our loveplay.

Rules of propriety forbade any demonstration of our affection except when we were alone. But they could not stop my eyes from seeking out my wife while I was bringing baskets of mulberry leaves into the family's silkwormhouse, taking out the waste to feed the fish in our ponds, or sitting in our courtyard, smoking, talking to my brothers, playing with their children. And on those occasions I was reckless enough to let my stolen glances linger on Bo See's wide, generous mouth, slender neck, sloping shoulders, delicate wrists, or long, supple fingers, the sparks of desire smoldering in me would crackle into blaze fast as a dry branch near a fire.

Once, about to stack dried mulberry branches in the kitchen for fuel, I chanced upon Bo See in the common room alone, setting up embroidery frames for herself and our sisters-in-law so they could begin their winter work. Usually the house was as crowded with family as it was cluttered with tools, large storage jars and sacks and baskets and chests. But Ba was in bed with a particularly bad attack of catarrh; Eldest Sister-in-law, exhausted from nursing him through the night, had been released to nap; Ma, now closeted with Ba, had told Second and Fourth Sisters-in-law to take outside any grandchild who wasn't in the fields with my brothers or in school; and Third Sister-in-law had been assigned to go buy embroidery thread from the waterpeddlers.

My first thought was to invite Bo See into our sleeping room for play. But the few rooms in our house had been divided, then subdivided, as each of my four brothers and I married. None of the flimsy wood partitions reached the ceiling, and our sleeping room was adjacent to Ba's.

Impulsively, I abandoned my chore, ripped off a button and, without removing my jacket, asked Bo See to sew it back on.

Her eyes glowing with a heat that matched my own, Bo See seized needle and thread, daringly suggested I unfasten the remaining buttons, murmuring, "That will make it easier."

Although the autumn day was cool, my chest gleamed moistly from my exertions, and when Bo See, piercing the edge of my jacket with her needle, let her wrist slide across my skin while pulling the thread through, I shivered with excitement. Her fingers trembling, she plunged the needle back into the fabric—stabbed her finger.

Except for a sharp intake of breath, she made no sound as she extracted the needle. But I took her injured hand in mine, placed the wounded finger in my mouth, embraced it with my lips, caressed it with my tongue.

Then she did cry out. It was only a small sob, one of pleasure, not pain. . . .

"Wai!"

Our faces bright as the sun outside, we leaped apart. At the other end of the common room, Third Sister-in-law—her shock clearly as great as our own—dropped the chest of embroidery thread she was carrying onto the table with a thud. Quickly, I shrugged off my jacket as if that was what I'd been doing all along, handed it to Bo See.

"Thanks, I won't wait," I mumbled, bolting out through the kitchen into the courtyard.

Panting as though I'd run in from the fields, I collapsed in an untidy heap. Our chickens, terrified, flapped and squawked a hasty retreat. Too edgy to stay still, I jumped up, began snapping the slender branches of mulberry into more manageable lengths for the stove.

As I piled the broken branches against my bare chest, I felt every scrape, prick, and stab from the rough bark and sharply pointed twigs. Welcoming the punishment, I heaped the sticks high, carried them into the kitchen.

From inside the common room, I could hear my wife and sister-in-law over the loud pounding of my heart: Bo See was stammering an increasingly muddled explanation, Third Sister-in-law giggling ever harder. Long before day's end, all four of our sisters-in-law and my brothers were laughing at us. Nor had they let up in the years since.

They were always joking that Bo See favored me while serving at meals. Then they'd twit me if I tried to defend her. They also teased whenever they saw us helping each other with a chore or if they caught me saving Bo See a slice of sweet fruit or bringing her a flower.

Our sisters-in-law once went so far as to ask Bo See, amidst titters, if the reason for our childlessness was because she drank from my rod. My brothers, no less bold, jovially advised me to stop weakening my seed through too frequent loveplay.

How Bo See and I envied women who openly lived together like husband and wife. These couples, as women, could express their affection for each other with the same impunity as good friends. No one raised so much as an eyebrow when they sat side-by-side, linked arms, or walked hand-in-hand in the streets, leaning into each other. Last year, one couple even decorated an altar to Gwoon Yum with love poems, then vowed before the Goddess, their kinfolk, and friends that they would never part.

Later, in the privacy of our sleeping room, Bo See and I had fed each other the couple's sweet bridal cakes and dreamtalked of enjoying similar freedom ourselves. Now, bound and gagged in the bottom of my kidnappers' boat, I vowed to Fook Sing Gung, the God of Luck, that if he helped restore me to my wife, I would be content with what we had, never again wish for more.

⌁

WHEN ACCOMPANYING BA or my brothers to market as a small boy, I could easily mark our journey by sounds and smells alone. Women's chatter, the laughter and cries of children, the slap of clothes against rock would signify we were passing a village, and after I counted three, I'd listen for the waterwheel's creak that marked the fork in the river. Then deliciously fragrant smoke from street vendors cooking over small clay stoves and the clash of cymbals, high-pitched fluting of pipes, and beating of gongs from street performers would herald our approach to town. Going home, the comforting aroma from the eucalyptus trees lining Strongworm's riverbank would foretell our arrival.

Imprisoned beneath the planking of my kidnappers' sampan, I realized that no matter how strong a smell managed to find its way through the cracks in the decking, the stink within would overpower it. And the dull throbbing in my head had long ago become a hammering that excluded all other sounds. I did, however, feel a series of jolts that suggested a poorly handled docking. Moments later, the board directly above my head rose into blinding light.

As I blinked, thick fingers dug into my arms and hauled me up. I didn't need sight to know it was the two strongmen who held me fast. Squinting, I made out a lantern swinging from the wizened, long-robed kidnapper's skeletal hand.

Suddenly, he lunged towards me, and in his lantern's glow, I caught the glimmer of a knifeblade. Shrinking within, I let out a shriek that died in a horrible gurgle behind my wooden gag and swollen tongue.

His lips spread in a malicious leer; his eyes glittered like the knifepoint he was aiming at my throat. Bearing down until I jerked at its sharpness, he hissed, "Give us any—I repeat *any* trouble, and this will be your fate."

"You don't understand, my sister will ransom me!"

But it was I who did not understand. For although he had ripped the wooden gag from my mouth, I couldn't utter anything louder or more articulate than strangled mewls. When he slashed the bindings from my wrists, my arms lacked any strength. Likewise, my feet and legs could not support me after they were freed.

Nor were we at a dock, as I had supposed, but alongside a vessel. I was forced to board by the strongmen lifting me from below while a pair above gripped my shoulders and arms, hoisted me over the side, and dragged me to an open hatch.

"Get below."

"Be quick about it!"

Mindful of my kidnapper's threat, I attempted to obey. But there was no lantern near, the moon in the night sky was young, and neither my eyes nor my benumbed feet could find a ladder.

The instant the strongmen released me, then, I fell. And the shock, the impact of ankles, knees, elbows, and skull hitting hardwood in quick succession was piercing.

In the pitch black hold, murmured warnings flitted like spirits.

"Move."

"Get out of the way."

"Hurry."

I tried but could not. Hands fumbled against my pants, grabbed a leg, a corner of my jacket, a sleeve, a shoulder, then pulled me deeper into the darkness just as a body, tumbling through the hatch, slammed the deck with a jarring thud, a garbled grunt.

There were more whispered warnings. Sounds of shuffling, dragging. Sobs. Faint groans that were somehow all the more awful for being muted.

Another body toppled down.

No sooner did flesh and bone thump then a heavy grate clanged over the hatch. While it was yet reverberating, a metal bolt rasped. As it locked into place, the sobs intensified, and it seemed to me I heard Bo See's cries as well as my own.

My father named me Bo See, Precious Silk, because I was born in a cocoonlike caul. But my family called me Bo Bo, Doubly Precious.

When matchmakers began approaching my parents with offers, my father refused to give them a hearing, saying, "I believe our Bo Bo has a nonmarrying fate." He even declared, "Once Bo Bo becomes a sworn spinster, I'll give her the rights of a son. While living, she can remain at home. After she dies, her spirit tablet will be placed on the family altar to be honored by future generations."

The rest of our family supported his proposal with an enthusiasm many a daughter would envy. Having become "Bo Bo" only after I had increased our profits, I understood my family's affection was more for my ability to raise healthy silkworms than for me. Besides, I wanted a husband to share my bed so I could have babies that would grow in my belly and suckle at my breasts.

To my relief, my father could not force me to become a sworn spinster. Those vows, a lifelong commitment to independence, must be made of a girl's free will. Unlike spinsters who can simply exchange baskets of peanut-candies, honey, and other sweets to signify their desire to live together as husband and wife, however, custom prevented me from arranging a marriage for myself. Nor could I compel my parents to find a husband for me.

Or could I?

THERE WERE TWO fortunetellers in our village, one blind and the other sighted. Each used a different method of augury: The blind man made careful calculations based on a person's month, day, and hour of birth; the sighted one divined fates with the help of a little black bird that he carried around in a dainty bamboo cage.

These fortunetellers operated in opposite corners of the temple courtyard. The blind man, on hearing a client's particulars, raised his gnarled fingers one by one, pursed his lips, and stroked his beard thoughtfully before issuing his pronouncements. The sighted man folded papers of obscure text that he tossed into the air and let fall helter-skelter. Then he pressed his already flat nose against the narrow bars of the bamboo cage and, directing his bird to show him his client's fate, he unlatched the gate.

Inside the cage, the bird would hop off its perch, flutter its wings, and fly through the opening. Once out, it might flit from paper to paper, study several with its head cocked, or select one instantly. Always, though, the bird would stab its beak between the folds of a paper, fly to its master, and the fortuneteller, unfolding the paper, would smooth out the creases, read the few lines of text out loud, and divine their meaning for that particular client.

I gave this fortuneteller two folded papers which required no interpretation beyond their color: white for the purity of spinsters; wedding red. I also ensured the bird's choice by hiding grain in the folds of the red.

After the fortuneteller decreed I had a marrying fate, my parents stopped turning away matchmakers. But my father set my bride price so high that had it not been for Moongirl's generoslty, I mlght yet be unwed and raising silkworms for his profit. Certainly I wouldn't have known the happiness of lying with Ah Lung, and I thanked the God of Luck daily for my good fortune.

My head leaden as the patch of sky overhead, I strove to piece together what little I'd noticed during my transfer from the sampan.

The strongmen who'd hauled me on board had merely leaned over the side. So the main deck couldn't be more than two or three feet above water. They'd taken maybe four strides to reach the hatch, which looked about two-and-a-half to three feet square. The gloom in the recesses of the hold made its size impossible to assess with any accuracy, but the muffled rumble of talk and fitful sobs within indicated the presence of many captives. So its length was likely several times its width, and its height had to be the same as the ladder I'd been unable to use last night: perhaps seven feet, at most eight.

Surely a vessel this slender and shallow was meant for rivers rather than oceans. Then it couldn't be a devil-ship, could it?

From the talk of the men within earshot, I knew the boat had been negotiating narrow channels and streams for days, picking up captives from isolated spots where there were no human sounds except their own. And during the night, the boat had dashed one way, then swung round to the sound of sails flapping, cracking taut, only to turn again after another glide, indicating we were still in the network of rivers that webbed the Pearl River Delta.

Since those pursuing the gentry's rewards for the capture of man-stealers were probably in these rivers, too, I'd prayed that the Goddess Gwoon Yum in her boat of mercy would guide these reward-seekers to save us. But for some time now the boat had not veered at all, and I feared we'd come to open sea and were beyond rescue.

If any of the men around me noted this change, they did not reveal it. Probably the two sharp-boned captives from the sampan couldn't yet speak any more than I, and with at least as many lumps and bruises as myself, they seemed absorbed in their discomfort, awkwardly shifting positions with throaty groans.

A young master wearing silk was huddled by the ladder, as he had been since daybreak. His eyes, swollen red, were leaking tears, and he was opening and shutting his bloodless lips like a hooked fish.

The air even slightly away from the grated hatch was thick and heavy, but the glare directly under it was fierce despite the sunless sky. Incredibly, the young master had a servant, an elderly man with stooped shoulders, who was hovering over him with a borrowed straw hat, waving it up and down, creating both shade and breeze—doubtless easing the smells of vomit, shit, and piss as well.

On the other side of the ladder squatted three gamblers and a morose man with wisps of gray hair sprouting from his chin. Earlier, these gamblers—Sleepy, Toothless, and Big Belly—had boasted to the morose graybeard that they could sniff out cardsharks. Now they were explaining how they'd come to follow a man-stealer onto a large hulk fitted up as a gambling hall.

"He was dressed as poorly as us," Toothless said.

"None of us had seen him before." Sleepy's eyelids drooped. Bracing his elbows on his knees, he supported his head with his hands and dragged out each word more slowly than the last. "We were strangers to each other, too."

"You know how it is," Big Belly cut in. "This man was offering three times the amount staked to whoever guessed the right number of seeds in the orange he held, and there was a big crowd around him. That's what caught my eye.

"Then the man offered me the orange to examine, and I couldn't pass up the chance for a big win. I'd been listening to everybody place their bets, see, and soon as I held that orange in my hands, I knew they'd guessed wrong. How? Because it was loose-skinned, and from my experience the looser the skin, the greater the number of seeds!"

Toothless snorted; Sleepy wheezed.

Big Belly slapped his oddly puny chest. "I won, didn't I?"

"If you call this winning, yeah," Sleepy drawled.

Toothless guffawed.

"Alright. Alright." Big Belly cracked his knuckles as though he wished they were the heads of those who mocked him. "So I believed that snake when he said he knew a place where I could double my winnings. But the two of you *begged* to come along."

Sleepy hung his head. Toothless mumbled something in a bitter tone. The morose graybeard sighed heavily. Because the gamblers' foolishness reminded him of his own? Or because our fates as piglets were sealed?

EVEN GIRLS WITH nonmarrying fates must follow the proper order of eldest to youngest in all things. So Moongirl, younger than my husband by almost an hour, had to wait until the autumn after Ah Lung and I married to make her vows of spinsterhood.

By custom, girls make these vows before Seh Gung, the Community Grandfather, whose altar is never in a temple but out in the open at the edge of a village. And because vows of spinsterhood include a commitment to lives of purity, girls making them scrub their faces and wear plain cotton jackets and pants instead of making themselves attractive like brides with powder, elaborate headdresses, and embroidered silks; the ceremony is held at first light when no man is yet abroad; only sworn spinsters and girls like themselves can attend.

Before my marriage, I'd witnessed two friends, Ah Gum and Ah Lan, make their vows. There'd been such a thick mist that the palms behind Seh Gung's stone altar had barely been visible, and our every breath had steamed in the chill. Shivering, I'd burrowed deeper into the huddle of witnesses while Ah Gum and Ah Lan, bustling between baskets and altar, unpacked, placed a small statue of the Goddess Gwoon Yum on Seh Gung's altar, and arranged offerings of wine, rice, and fruit. Then they set out candles and incense and lit them.

Unlike brides who have someone else transform their girlish bangs and braids into womanly buns, girls who become spinsters ceremonially comb up their hair themselves to signify their independence. For days, I'd watched Ah Lan and Ah Gum practice. Now, as waxy, fragrant smoke from the candles and incense wafted up to Heaven, they each nimbly unfastened their braids, letting loose ribbons of black hair that shone in the flames' glow.

Three times they ran their combs from scalp to waist and, in voices smooth and strong as each stroke, asked for Heaven's blessings: "First comb, comb to the end. Second comb, may my brother enjoy bountiful wealth and many children. Third comb, may my parents and friends enjoy wealth, happiness, and long life."

Then, dipping their fingers into a jar of sticky pow fa, they applied just the right amount to hold together their hair for braiding, weaving, and pinning. The final strands and pins in place, they vowed to remain unmarried and pure, sought the blessings and protection of Seh Gung and Gwoon Yum, turned to receive our congratulations. Afterward, we celebrated at a banquet that was paid for by their families and included relatives and neighbors as well as friends.

The dishes served at such banquets are not costly. But Moongirl's parents, having spent the last of her savings on a wedding banquet for Ah Lung and myself, could not even purchase the long buns that families pass out as invitations. And although Moongirl, in the silk season just past, had earned enough as a reeler to pay for a banquet, she had other plans for her money.

I WAS WAKENED by a sense of movement and mutterings in the hold, shouts from above. Rubbing away the sleep crusting my eyes, I peered up at the hatch. The grating was gone, and against a star-studded sky was a face too shadowed to make out, a narrow, swift-moving blur that vanished with the unmistakable thwack of a cane, another harsh shout: "Up on deck!"

Around me, the activity intensified, stirring up particular odors from the general stench. The air scraped my parched throat like sand, and I became aware of the furriness of my tongue, still tender and somewhat swollen, the bitter aftertaste of yesterday's rice flavored with shrimp paste. I realized the boat was at anchor.

"Fai-dee-ah, hurry!"

Someone started up the ladder. Others stumbled after him. Frightened by what awaited us above as well as stiff and sore, I dragged myself upright but made no move to follow.

From somewhere beyond the boat came a plaintive call, "Ah Jai, son! Ah Jai!"

Crying, "Ba," Young Master dashed up the ladder.

More swiftly than I'd thought possible, his elderly servant likewise disappeared through the hatch, setting off a rush for the ladder, a buzz of speculation. How had Young Master's father found him? Was he a man of sufficient generosity and influence to secure freedom for the rest of us, too?

Shoved deep into the hold, I could no longer hear anything except tramping feet, and I fretted that Young Master's father would only save those he could see, that he and those he rescued would be long gone before I reached the deck. I berated myself for having hung back, I wondered whether we were someplace where Moongirl might also know to come and ransom me. Certainly we couldn't be in a foreign land, not this fast, could we?

Finally able to throw myself onto the ladder behind Big Belly, I seized what felt like a rung.

"Wai!" Big Belly protested.

Recognizing my mistake, I released his sandaled feet, fumbled for the sides of the ladder, made my ascent.

As my head poked through the hatch, fresh salt air swirled over me, cleansing. Another two steps and the stuffy heat of the hold gave way to pre-dawn cool, making me shiver; I was struck blind by a blaze of lanterns.

Desperate to adjust my eyes so I could find Young Master and his father, I halted and blinked.

A hand whipped out, snatched my queue, hauled me up the ladder's final rungs. "Didn't I say hurry?"

At the hot spikes of pain shooting through my skull and neck, I howled, earning a stinging cuff to my ear that would have knocked me over were it not for the strongman's grip on my queue. Deafened, I staggered, hoping Young Master and his father would appear in the flashes of captives, masts, Sleepy slouching through the hatch onto the deck. . . .

Another vicious yank on my queue jerked me to a standstill, and in the moment it took me to see I was again behind Big Belly, the strongman grabbed my wrists and wound the gambler's long, wiry braid around them with an expertise born of practice. From the sharp tugs at the nape of my neck, I understood Sleepy was likewise being bound with my hair.

The shackling completed, my arms were bent at the elbow; my hands, raised high as my chest, were folded together as if in supplication. Except for my legs, I could not move without affecting the other men in line, all similarly tethered, and as we were herded ashore, my view was limited to Big Belly's broad back, the gangplank groaning beneath our feet.

~

ON THE BOAT, the strongmen and captives around me had spoken either my district dialect or Saang Wah, the city dialect that I was familiar with through merchants and

Moongirl. Since the metal door of the pigpen had slammed behind us, however, I'd understood almost no one. The room, although cavernous, was packed with men, most speaking dialects I'd never before heard, and no sooner had a brawny guard unshackled me from my fellow captives then I'd lost them in the muddle. Furthermore, the din was terrible. My head felt as if it would burst from the roar of talk and inexplicable explosions of firecrackers coupled with the loud beating of gongs, my heart.

Adding to my distress, the room's six barred windows were sealed with grimy oystershell panes that filtered out most of the light from the sun but none of the heat. I dripped sweat from every pore. With no fresh air coming in to diffuse the firecrackers' acrid fumes, my eyes and nose stung; my chest tightened.

Suddenly, guards armed with clubs began rounding up men, prodding and beating the reluctant. As I tried to avoid them, others—in their own efforts to escape— pushed me into the dragnet, and I found myself driven through a side door, up a long flight of stairs.

In the crush, all I could see were the queues, necks, and shoulders directly ahead, none of which I recognized. But the incessant jabbing from the pair I was wedged between reminded me of the sharp-boned captives in the sampan. While together in the hold, I'd noted their strong resemblance to each other and their obvious difference in age, guessed them to be father and son. Could this reminder of them be a sign from Heaven that I'd soon see Ba?

As if in confirmation, the fug from the bodies closing me in lessened the higher we rose. By the top of the stair-case, I was drawing deliciously clear breaths, and although we were crammed in a narrow hallway, my chest started to unclog; the pounding in my head eased.

Then we were spilling through double doors into a spa-cious room that was startlingly bright. Quiet, too. And no wonder: Before us loomed a giant of a foreign devil. He was so tall that his swarthy, beak-nosed face rose above the heads of all the men milling in the thirty or more feet between us!

Behind him, a door swung open, and a sallow-faced creature hurried in. While the giant was in some sort of uniform boasting shiny gold buttons and countless loops of gleaming braid, this creature wore a crumpled, ill-fit-ting, black western suit, and he scuttled across the pol-ished wood floor like a spider.

Halting beside the giant, who acknowledged his arrival with a magisterial nod, the spider threw back his shoul-ders, thrust out his chest, and reeled off an endless string of Saang Wah in a voice that was unexpectedly rich and deep. Soon multiple translations were rippling among the forty, fifty men in the room.

To my surprise, the giant made no effort to silence the talkers. Nor did the spider, and the distraction from this buzz coupled with the spider's speed made me unsure whether I understood him correctly.

I was fairly certain of the beginning: the spider had declared himself the right hand of the giant, who was an official, a very important mandarin of Macao, a Portuguese settlement at the mouth of the Pearl River. But was the spider now saying that this mandarin, like the famous iron-faced Magistrate Bau, was impartial and honest, that his presence was a guarantee we'd be treated fairly in this room, which was a hiring hall?

Men in every direction started calling out, and from what I could catch, they were begging for work. The giant—iron-faced like Magistrate Bau—did not so much as flick an eyelash. The spider, aided by wild gesticulations, launched into a glowing account of pay: four silver dollars per month above and beyond free room and board as well as two suits of clothing, one flannel shirt, and a new blanket every year.

At these generous terms, some men grew nearly as animated as the spider. But no amount of riches could tempt me from returning to my family and village, everything familiar, as soon as I could.

Skeptics shouted:

"Where is this work?"

"What is it?"

"What if I don't like it?"

The spider, raising his voice above theirs, boomed,

"This work is not far away but in Peru, a country of much gold and silver that can be reached in a few days sail. So if you don't like the work, you can easily quit and go home using the dollars you receive for signing on."

Extracting a little sack from a pants' pocket, he jiggled it, creating a happy clink of coins. "The advance is eight *silver* dollars, one for each year of the contract, each *foreign* year, which has just six months to our twelve."

He snapped his fingers. "Your time will be up that quick!"

Men ran towards him, clamoring:

"Give me a contract!"

"I'll sign!"

"I'll give you my thumbprint!"

Caught in the stampede, I was thrown against those ahead, pressed from behind, jammed in so tightly that my every attempt to wriggle free failed. Still I persisted, and those I jostled muttered incomprehensibly, cursed, demanded I wait my turn.

"I don't want a contract," I spluttered in my dialect, then in Saang Wah. "Let me out."

"What a muk tau, woodenhead!"

"You want the silver dollars, don't you?"

I hesitated. Since I'd been brought here through deceit, why shouldn't I sign falsely? Then I'd get the advance, which would not only buy my passage home but leave me with a small windfall to give Ba.

He had named me Yuet Lung, Moon Dragon, and my sister Yuet Fung, Moon Phoenix, to commemorate our birth during a full moon and to express his hope that we'd prove the saying, "Dragon and phoenix twins bring their families luck."

Ma said we had; Ba agreed. But I'd not needed the teasing of my brothers and sisters-in-law to recognize it had been Moongirl's money that had brought us my wife, and it was Bo See's extraordinary skill in raising silkworms that made it possible for our family to continue eating twice a day.

With the spider's silver dollars, I would have a chance to justify our parents' claim for myself, and I imagined my family's pleasure over my return, their surprise when my baby niece, leaping into my arms, made the coins in my jacket pocket jingle. As I brought out the silver dollars one by one, she'd clap her chubby hands in glee. Bo See would flush with pride. "Wah!" our other nieces and nephews and their parents would marvel. "Ho yeh, great!" When I placed the money in Ba's callused palms, his eyes, dulled by years of worry, would brighten; Ma's shoulders would lose some of their hunch. Bo See, at our family altar, would light incense to Heaven in gratitude, and we'd gift the son we'd make together with the name Ah Fook, Good Fortune.

⌐

IN OUR DISTRICT, ordinary people were reluctant to petition the magistrate for help lest their troubles deepen.

But the great Magistrate Bau, unlike our magistrate, was said to be as incorruptible as he was just, as attentive to the poor as to the rich. Even a lowly peanut-oil peddler once reported the theft of his earnings to Magistrate Bau and petitioned him to find the culprit.

This peddler couldn't describe the thief, and a thorough search for evidence by the magistrate's lieutenants turned up none. But Magistrate Bau, undaunted, made dozens of advertisements for "The Judgment of the Stone," a spectacle that could be viewed for a copper.

That very day, his lieutenants posted the notices around town. Everybody wanted to see the phenomenon, and as they poured into the magistrate's court, a lieutenant invited each person to drop their copper into a large pot of water with a stone at the bottom.

Coin after coin splashed into the water, sank, hit stone, and Magistrate Bau, standing beside the pot, watched carefully. But his iron-face never changed a jot. Not even when a sheen of oil suddenly appeared and he intoned, "The stone has judged."

In response, two lieutenants pounced on the man who'd thrown in the oily copper, causing more oil-streaked coins to fall out of his pockets. When accused of stealing them from the peanut-oil peddler, however, the man insisted he had not. Why? Because a suspect has to confess before he can be sentenced, and the man knew from Magistrate Bau's reputation that he was too honest to break the law.

Magistrate Bau, though, was as relentless as he was honest and clever. So he ordered the man tortured, and after the application of both finger *and* ankle screws, the thief confessed.

Then and only then did Magistrate Bau pass sentence.

In the Macao hiring hall, I took note of how closely the iron-faced giant watched each man as he responded to the spider's query, "Are you willing to go overseas to work?" And I started having questions of my own. If the iron-faced giant resembled Magistrate Bau in brilliance and determination as well as appearance, wouldn't he somehow divine I was signing a contract just to get the advance? Instead of countersigning it, wouldn't he denounce me, order me tortured if I tried to deny the lie?

Much as I wanted the silver dollars for my family, I would not risk my freedom for cash. So when my turn came, I answered honestly, "No."

"Wah, what a joker!" Clapping me on the back, the man to my left called on those around us to bring me to my senses.

Their response was rapid and strong.

"Don't be a fool."

Afraid the giant would be angered by the commotion and blame me, I loudly repeated, "No!"

To my relief, the spider beckoned a guard, ordered him to escort me out.

I wanted nothing more than to quit the pigpen as fast as I could, to put the horror of the last few days behind me. But I was still bruised from my fall into the hold, and when the guard and I reached the stairs, I was wary of doing myself more damage by tumbling down. The guard, a brutish lout, spewed oaths at my cautious descent, quickened my step with his club.

After the spacious cool of the hiring hall, the suffocating heat, noise, and disorder of the pigpen hit me with the force of another blow. More captives were pouring in through the main door, and as the guard—forging a narrow opening in the crowd—led me in a different direction, I prayed I'd get outside before my head shattered like the long strings of exploding firecrackers.

My eyes teared from the pungent smoke. When we came to another set of stairs, I grasped the banister and stumbled down blindly. At the bottom, I smeared my eyes dry with my knuckles—discovered what the prolonged blasts of firecrackers, deep drumrolls, and brassy gongs were hiding from passersby, the captives upstairs.

My hands flew up again to cover my eyes. But I could not shut out the anguished shrieks of those being beaten with the flats of swords, the smelly splatter of human waste cascading from privy holes overhead onto men caged below. Thanking Heaven I'd not lied and was free to leave, I separated my fingers, peered through the slots for the guard who was guiding me out.

He was approaching a man bound by his thumbs to a beam overhead. The man's toes touched the floor, but barely, certainly without the purchase necessary to ease the torture of the cord and, his face twisted with pain, he was bleating piteously.

The guard, yanking the cord tying the man to the beam, jacked his feet into the air, jolting from him a piercing wail.

"*Now* are you willing to labor overseas?" the guard sneered.

I realized then the hiring hall was a sham, the iron-faced giant corrupt, and my chest cleaved open; my mind raced like a cornered rat. How long could I withstand torture? And to what end? Were those who insisted, "No, I won't go," tortured to death? What about those who became too injured to work? Were they released? Could I, as a cripple, make my way home?

At home, we had to raise thousands of worms during the long silk season. How could I return a cripple and burden my family with a useless mouth to feed?

MY SISTER-IN-LAW'S earnings from embroidery and reeling silk had covered my bride price because Moongirl was skillful in both. Fashioning the hair of friends and family into the elegant styles depicted in pictures of highborn ladies, Moongirl proved as clever at wielding a comb, and she preferred it.

Nobody in a village hires hairdressers except for weddings, however, and then the woman, doubling as a dai kum, bridal escort, has to be the mother of sons, many sons, in hopes that the bride, too, will have sons. Even the wives of landlords and gentry don't have their hair combed by an outside person but by their maids.

In cities, though, wealthy women favor more elaborate styles, and they hire hairdressers to come to their homes. At night, these ladies hold their heads off their beds by resting their necks on narrow pillows of cool porcelain. Nevertheless, they usually find it necessary to have their hair redone every few days.

Moongirl, as an independent spinster, required no one's permission to leave Strongworm for the city. But she realized her actions reflected on both her family and her sister spinsters, and a move to Canton would be marked by every eye and tongue in the village since no woman in Strongworm had ever traveled beyond the market town. Hoping to deflect criticism, protect her own modesty, and ensure her success, Moongirl asked the abbess of the largest nunnery in the market town, Ten Thousand Mercies Hall, to help her.

When Moongirl told the family, my brothers-in-law and their wives chortled. Under his breath, Ah Lung admitted to me that had Moongirl not discussed her intentions and reasoning with us, he would have laughed, too.

If their amusement ruffled Moongirl, she did not show it.

"Did I hear you right?" Third Brother-in-law goaded. "You asked a woman who shaves her head to help you become a hairdresser?"

His wife, the rest of our sisters-in-law and their husbands laughed harder. Even so, Moongirl's square face remained placid. Nor did she attempt an explanation. But Ba glowered, thwarting any further teasing, smothering the smallest titter.

"The abbess is from the largest clan in our village *and* she's the head of this district's most important nunnery," he reminded.

"*Can* Rooster help you?" Ma worried out loud.

At her mother's use of the abbess's childhood name, Moongirl smiled. "Two of her nuns will accompany me to

Canton on a boat operated by women. And one of the nunnery's largest donors contacted her cousin, a wealthy widow
by the name of Choy Tai, in the city. Choy Tai has arranged
respectable quarters for me to rent. She's also promised to
hire me to comb her hair and introduce me to her friends."

As she spoke, Ma beamed relief, Ba pride, Ah Lung and I
our support. And when Moongirl finished, there were no
naysayers, only praise:

"Ho yeh, great!"

"You're as clever with your head as your hands!"

WHEN THE GUARD returned me to the airy upstairs hall, I noticed the morose graybeard and the three gamblers among the new group of captives. Ducking my head, I skulked away from them like a beaten dog; The guard had threatened to kill me should I expose the hoax to anyone, even inadvertently, and in my jangled state, I feared I might. Once again there were demands for work. I thought I recognized the callers' voices, and stealthy glances at their faces revealed they were the same men who'd taken the lead before. My eyes bulging, I observed their manipulations and realized these men weren't captives but hirelings, hirelings charged with helping the spider to lure us the way Bo See did silkworms.

Our family used to transfer our worms from dirty paper onto clean by brushing them with a quill. Of course we were careful. But many of the worms—no thicker than a thread when hatched—would be injured anyway. Bo See showed us how to place one side of a soiled sheet at the edge of a fresh piece on which she'd spread finely cut mulberry so the worms, attracted by the smell of the leaves, would quit the old paper of their own volition, crawling unharmed onto the new.

As the spider flashed silver dollars before us, I heard Big Belly gloating to Toothless and Sleepy, "See? I did win." And the morose graybeard—apparently fearful his age would deny him the chance of a contract—fashioned a turban out of his jacket, and used it to cover the scraggly gray queue coiled around his crown. He pinched one of his frail whiskers between two gnarled fingers, yanked it out with a startled little yelp, a sudden watering of his rheumy eyes, and resolutely fumbled for another betraying hair.

He was still plucking, squealing and squeaking with each whisker, when one of the hirelings nudged me in front of the spider with a jovial, "Your turn."

"Are you willing to go overseas?" the spider asked.

More jangled than ever, I scarcely managed a nod.

"Name?"

As I struggled to unknot my tongue, the hireling joked, "Better hurry or I'll jump queue," stirring laughter, a wave of goodnatured, "Fai-dee-ah, hurry."

"W-w-wong Yuet Lung," I stammered.

The spider scrawled the characters. "Age and district?"

"T-twenty-four. Sun Duk."

Turning the contract so it faced me, the spider jabbed a long-nailed finger at the space next to a ream of words, only the last of which I had a chance to read: "This contract has been explained in full, and I freely and spontaneously agree to bind myself to labor obediently in Peru for eight years, the time to count from the day I begin to work."

Jogged by the hireling, I grasped the brush, dipped the bristles into the black puddle at the center of the inkstone. But I could not make myself write my name.

"Let me help you, brother," the hireling said.

Snatching the brush, he inked my thumb and pressed it onto the paper as if I'd not attended school for almost three years but was completely illiterate. Then he passed the contract to the giant for countersigning.

⁓

IN THE JUNK that ferried us from the quay to the devil-ship, we were locked below.

The spider had warned us that it would be necessary lest the unscrupulous among us disappear. "You'll also have to walk to the quay shackled and guarded by soldiers with muskets."

Skillfully, the hirelings had cut off protesters:

"That's fair. We've been given a lot of money."

"Yeah, I understand."

One tipped his head meaningfully at the iron-faced giant.

"Better shackles and armed guards than have Magistrate Bau catch us running."

Many in the hall shuddered, grunted agreement.

"You can bet he'd turn a runaway over to his lieutenants for a lashing."

"Or worse."

The morose graybeard, no longer morose or bearded, rattled the silver coins in his pocket. "I'm glad for the soldiers and their muskets. They'll protect our money from thieves."

The biggest thieves, though, were our captors, who sold us supplies—everything from tobacco to blankets—at four, maybe five times their value.

My last taste of tobacco had been the morning I was kidnapped. Cradling my longstemmed pipe, I'd breathed in the delicate yet distinctive scent of Bo See along with the smoke's fragrance, and as its heat had coursed through me, I'd savored again the red-hot pleasuring we'd shared on waking. Since then, I'd lost every trace of Bo See's scent in the accumulated stink. My jacket and pants, crusted with filth, crackled, and I yearned for a wash and change of clothes as much as a smoke.

Even more, I longed for Bo See. So I made no purchases. Instead I vowed I'd spend every copper of my eight silver dollars on sacrifices to Fook Sing Gung if he'd come to my aid and show me a way home.

EMERGING ONTO THE junk's deck, we were surrounded by foul-mouthed strongmen, ringed so tightly we couldn't spread our legs for balance, and we teetered and rocked as the junk heaved in long swells. The soldiers that had been guarding us since we left the pigpen remained, their muskets at the ready. But the hirelings had melted away, and without their misleading patter, there was plenty of grousing, some of it black as the devil-ship alongside. Yet my own mood lightened. For the devil-ship's hull rose much higher than the junk's deck, and it seemed to me that any gangway between the two would have to be steeply raked, making it doubtful we'd be fettered together for the climb. Furthermore, the plank being set up looked barely wide enough for a pair of feet, too narrow for the unwilling to be dragged aboard.

Already I could see myself mounting the gangplank, studying my feet as if I intended climbing to the devil-ship with every care. A couple of small steps, and I'd feel hot sun on my crown, know I was leaving the gloomy shadow cast by the devil-ship's hull. Another two or three, and I'd gulp a mouthful of moist, salt-laden air, buckle my knees, and tumble from the heat into the sea's cool embrace.

A bellowed order for us to face the shore snapped me back. But I offered up a quick prayer of thanks as I turned towards the bellower: a short, powerfully built man with small, close-set eyes. Nor was I discouraged when Small Eyes, his voice dripping spite, pointed out how the stone buildings at the quay, although double-and-triple storied, seemed the size of huts because they were so far away. Yes, we were in the outer harbor, which was crowded with tall-masted foreign vessels, and it had been years since I'd been in water except to wash. But I'd swum great distances as a boy. Moreover, junks and sampans littered the glittering jade-green water. Surely they didn't all serve man-stealers like the junk we were on. If I floundered during the swim, one with sympathetic boatmen would save me, perhaps even carry me home.

"Man-eating sharks live in these waters. What's more, the devil-captains offer standing rewards for the return of anybody foolish enough to jump. The jumpers don't have to be brought back alive or whole. A single limb will do."

Determined not to fall victim to another hoax, I stopped listening to Small Eyes and began mapping a course to shore. If I took the most direct route, there'd be four foreign vessels in my path. Each had a garish foreign God or Goddess carved on its prow, and any one of them might be a devil-ship, but the heads, even the decks, rose high above the water, so neither their Gods nor their crews seemed likely to notice me. Butting up against their hulls, however, were sampans, their boatmen shouting offers of wares, rides to the quay. Junks, too, plied back and forth, some so

weighed down by cargo that the large, all-seeing eyes painted on their prows almost touched the water. Perhaps I
should avoid the risk of discovery by going underwater like
a waterbrave.

The waterbraves who'd fought against the devil-foreigners
in the first opium war had been renowned for their reckless
courage in the face of danger, and they had among them
astonishing divers who could walk on the seafloor for hours
on end. As children, Moongirl and I had worked long and
hard at emulating them, and we'd learned to keep our toes
from stirring up a single thread of the streambed's soft silt,
to glide without moving our arms and legs or leaking a
trace of air. . . .

"Piglet overboard!"

The alarm, repeated many times over, did not come
from our junk or the devil-ship alongside. But our cordon
of strongmen immediately tightened their noose; the soldiers stiffened; Small Eyes dashed to the side.

Pinched together, we trampled each other's feet, our
sweat-soaked clothes and skin melded as one. Worse, men
were yelling instructions to pursuers from every direction,
Small Eyes was taking wagers from the crew on whether
the jumper would be caught dead or alive. Did a jumper
have absolutely *no* chance of success?

Stretching my neck, I ogled over shoulders and between
heads in search of someplace the jumper might seek refuge
besides the faraway quay—saw a foreign vessel with a face

as unadorned and compassionate as Gwoon Yum's carved on its prow. If the jumper swam to this ship, perhaps the crew crowding its side would take pity on him.

There were no sampans around its hull that would block his way, no junks nearby, and from the few skiffs hovering close came haunting cries rather than shouted instructions from the chase. Or were the cries echoes from seabirds screeching at the black head bobbing in the shallow dip of a golden-green swell?

These traitorous birds, swooping low, were acting like a beacon to the boatmen in pursuit, and the jumper, despite frantic paddling, was making little progress. With a horrible sinking sensation, I realized there was every reason I'd fare as badly.

Moongirl and I had swum in a stream that was four or five feet at its deepest, and I'd never experienced a river's current let alone a sea's. Moreover, waterplay had ended for us at the age of seven, when I'd started school and Moongirl had begun laboring in earnest, so we'd never been hampered by clothing while swimming.

Watching the jumper, I felt his struggle as though it were my own, and as the sampans gained on him, I silently urged, *Dive! Dive now!*

His head did vanish. But was it intentional?

Maybe I'd just lost sight of him in the swells.

Or he could be hidden by the sampans that had converged.

If he *was* swimming underwater, was he deep enough to elude the tangle of grappling hooks and nets the boatmen were now hurling?

The answer came in a triumphant, "We've caught the piggy!"

"He's a goner," Small Eyes boomed.

So, it seemed, was I.

THE DAY MY husband disappeared in the market town, some Strongworm spinsters recognized our family skiff tied up near theirs, overheard Fourth Brother-in-law frantically seeking information about Ah Lung from people nearby.

Joining the search, these spinsters spread out along the riverbank. One of them came across eyewitnesses to a fight in which two strongmen had bested a victim fitting Ah Lung's description, and she readily agreed to return the family's skiff to us and break the dreadful news while Fourth Brother-in-law caught a fastboat for Canton to inform Moongirl.

From what Moongirl had said about the city's dangers, Fourth Brother-in-law could be kidnapped, too. Ma's wrinkled face turned gray as her hair; Fourth Sister-in-law started wailing like a widow. I roiled within as though I were back in the cramped, windowless bridal sedan that had brought me to Ah Lung.

Merely looking at wares on a waterpeddler's boat made me queasy, and since my bride escort had warned me that we'd have to cross a river to reach Strongworm, I'd knotted a salted plum into my hankerchief to settle my stomach during our passage. Almost immediately, however, the sedan's rocking upset me. Or perhaps it was the smoke from the firecrackers that had blown into the sedan before my escort locked me in, the mounting stuffiness and heat, the oily heaviness of the traditional sticky rice I'd eaten at my final meal with my family.

In the dark, I fumbled for something to hang onto, found one hemp loop, then another, and clutched them so tightly my nails bit into my palms. Still, I jounced on the sedan's narrow bench, and only chewing the plum's salty meat quieted the churning within. By the time I heard the sedan bearers shout for a boatman, I was down to the pit.

Suddenly the bearer in front—despite my escort's urgent admonitions to take care boarding the ferry—lost his footing, and I swung off the bench entirely, wrenching my shoulders.

To my relief, there was no splash of water and I regained my seat. In a confusing clamor of curses, accusations, and misdirections, though, I hurtled backwards, thwacking my head, knocking askew my headdress and veil.

Even after the sedan thumped onto the decking, it dipped alarmingly. I pressed the pit from the plum against the roof of my mouth with my tongue, and as the ferry rose, dipped, rose again, I sucked down so hard I tasted blood. But I could not stop my stomach from convulsing, shooting sour vomit into my mouth, and I'd had to rip my right hand from its loop of hemp and clap my hankerchief to my lips—like I did just moments ago, on learning kidnappers held my husband captive.

Now, forcing myself to swallow, I sought to calm all by turning the family's attention from what we could not know for certain to what we did.

Moongirl combed her patrons' hair with perfumed oils, secured their elaborate coifs with decorative pins of silver and gold. Sometimes she also plucked unwanted hairs from her patrons' faces, painted their lips, colored their nails with a paste made from crushed red petals steeped in alum. And as she combed, plucked, and painted, Moongirl would offer appropriate pleasantries or commiseration in response to her patrons' gossip and confidences. Pleased by her apparent interest and obvious skill, many of Moongirl's patrons encouraged her to linger after she had finished by offering her snacks, some tea. They included her in banquets, invited her to accompany them on excursions to temples and theaters or moon-viewings from rivers and lakes. Some of these patrons were the wives of men in positions of power, and Moongirl would surely seek their help in finding and ransoming Ah Lung, bringing him home.

As a son, I'd always been assured of my place in family and village: Not only did I know all fifty-one families, but through my father, who'd known their fathers, I was as familiar with their ancestors as my own. Torn from them, I felt completely unmoored.

Moongirl, though, had been taught from infancy that daughters cannot remain at home. To prepare for her inevitable departure, she'd had to start passing her nights in a girls' house when she was nine, and she'd been drilled in the weeping songs that brides chant to release their sorrow on leaving family and friends forever to live among strangers. Since Moongirl had chosen independent spinsterhood, she'd had no occasion to lament for herself. But she'd wailed on behalf of friends, and as I dragged my feet up the gangplank to the devil-ship, I could hear her chanting:

"Savages have taken you prisoner.

Once you . . ."

At the sound of her voice, a lump formed in my throat that I could neither raise nor swallow: The family knew I'd been kidnapped, and my sister had found me! By lamenting instead of calling my name, however, I understood Moongirl was warning that although she'd come to ransom me, my chances of rescue were as unlikely as those of an unwilling bride. My head became so heavy my chin sank onto my chest; the grime on my sandaled feet blurred with the planking. Stumbling on board, my head fell back. My eyes, slitted against the glare, swept up the masts until their tips vanished in a blaze of copper sky. Devil-foreigners swarmed across the spars, and I guessed from the intensity of their activity, the staccato footfalls on deck, sharply raised voices, shrill whistles, and clank of chains that the ship was about to get underway.

I scolded myself for not taking a chance and letting myself fall off the gangplank into the sea, swimming like mad until I found Moongirl. Now, hemming me in on both sides were devil-foreigners with gleaming swords threatening to scream across my skin, and I could do nothing except trudge between them.

When I came to a ladder, I mounted it. At the top, more devil-foreigners armed with muskets guarded the sides, the captives standing in three mute, disconsolate rows. My skin crawled with gooseflesh as I realized the muskets were fitted with bayonets. But I comforted myself with the hope that Moongirl, whom I could no longer hear, had gone to seek my release and, despite her warning, she'd secure my freedom. After all, on the boat this morning, Young Master's father had won his.

"Get in line," snapped a middle-aged Chinese devil in crisp, black-gummed silk.

This devil had a large black umbrella that shaded him from the brutal sun, yet his skin resembled melting wax. Having no umbrella nor hat, sweat ran down my face, chest, and back in rivers. As I walked across the hot deck, a disturbing rumble boiled up from below; pitch oozed from the planks' seams, gripping the soles of my sandals.

"Only ten across! Start a new row. No talking."

Obeying, I recognized the pointy ears of a scrawny, bare-chested fellow who'd refused to set foot on the gangplank. He hadn't been the first. A few had pleaded dizziness from the movement of the junk, and Small Eyes— who'd demonstrated how we should ascend the gangplank—had thrown down ropes from the devil-ship and ordered these captives hoisted aboard as if they were, in truth, pigs.

This fellow had not begged but hawked gobs of spit at the strongmen, then raged at our captors. Even after he'd been bound by his wrists and ankles and the devils hoisting him had deliberately slammed him so hard against the hull that I'd recoiled from the crack, he hadn't stopped shouting.

After he'd disappeared over the side, there'd been a single drawn-out cry, nothing more. And where there'd been some before him who keened or cursed their fate as they walked up the gangplank, those who followed, myself included, had been stone silent.

Now the pointy-eared resister, shackled at his wrists and ankles to a pair of iron rings bolted into the deck, had his head forcibly bowed. His back, badly shredded, was black with blood and swarms of mosquitoes and flies so sated they could scarcely crawl.

Clearly the devils had whipped him cruelly. Just as clearly, the devils had placed him in irons where we could see him for the same reason magistrates parade prisoners in heavy cangues: to add public humiliation to the punishment, and to frighten others into obedience.

What held my gaze, though, were the resister's fingers doubled over into fists.

❧

NO SOONER WERE we pigs assembled then six more devils crowded onto the stern deck. In the lead was a bloated sausage whose skin was almost as red as the hair bristling above his sea-green eyes, springing out of his oversized ears and nostrils, covering his head and jowls, the backs of his meaty hands. From the way this red devil swaggered, I thought he was the captain. But the interpreter, a muddy-faced mess of tics and twitches, told us the red devil was second-in-command of the ship. The colorless, clean-shaven reed with no neck and a head that listed to one side was the ship's doctor, the three barefoot devils common sailors, the Chinese in black-gummed silk our headman.

"Swineherd, you mean."

Were it not for the puff of breath on the back of my neck from the man behind me and the muffled snorts of those nearby, I would have mistaken this comment, quiet as it was bitter, for my own imagining. There was no mistaking Red's snarl though, and the interpreter, despite his tics and twitches, spoke distinctly, his translation in three dialects rising above birdcalls, the persistent eerie rumbling, the myriad noises from boat traffic and the devils clearing the main deck.

"Take off your clothes, including your hats and shoes, and put them on the deck. Those of you with belongings, place them on the deck as well. If you have your queue coiled around your head, release it so it hangs down your back."

Stuffing my silver dollars into my mouth for safekeeping, I started unbuttoning my jacket. Around me, men shed their hats and jackets and uncoiled their queues. Those who'd made purchases in the pigpen set down their bundles.

None that I could see reached for his pants' wide waistband. Nor would I. Since Moongirl and I had become too old for Ma to bathe us together in our courtyard, no one had seen me naked out in the open. Why would I degrade myself by stripping for this devil?

"Cooperate fully," the interpreter urged. "Any man the doctor finds diseased, addicted to opium, crippled, or too young or too old for labor will be set free."

A doctor—even one with a crooked head—could surely make those determinations while we were clothed! One glance at the morose graybeard's withered skin revealed his age, and from my neighbor's sunken eyes and hollow cheeks, it was obvious he was an addict.

Red, roaring so loud he shut out all else, clamped his meaty hands over the ears of the closest captive and lifted him into the air. Stunned by the devil's strength, I almost choked on my silver dollars. The interpreter twitched over to the swineherd, who looked on expressionless as Red, still roaring like an angry bull, dashed the poor sod onto the deck, ripped off his pants.

Burning inside now as fiercely as out, I stared at the deck to spare myself and my fellow captives the worst of our shame—dropped my pants. As I stepped out of them, then my sandals, onto scorching planks, I saw the men in front of me doing likewise. I also saw the doctor's form-fitting trousers and leather shoes hurry past the first row of bare legs and feet while Red circled each captive.

Every one of these men jumped, some with shocked gasps, many with furious belches and hisses. Fearful of what the devil was doing, I clenched my teeth against the moment he'd reach me.

The silver dollars mashed against the roof of my mouth, my tongue, and my gorge rose in protest at their weight, their unpleasant metallic taste. But there was nowhere else to hide them. The sailors were ransacking our clothes and bundles, sending silver dollars and strings of coppers flying, along with chopsticks, tobacco, pipes, tongue scrapers, preserved fruit. One of these devils, an oaf with eagles and stars painted on his forearms, was even sneaking coins into his own pockets.

Each time any of them came upon an opium pipe, tin of opium, earscoop, knife, or razor, they'd throw it aside. Occasionally Red, growling like a cur who'd snatched another dog's bone, would toss a razor, metal pick, or knife into the growing pile of confiscated items, too. The men he was circling, though, were naked. So where had Red found these items?

Suddenly meaty fingers were probing my armpits, tearing at my hair, poking into places where only Bo See's hands belong. Shaken to the core, I would have lost my dollars had it not been for my tightly clenched jaws.

Then the fingers were pinching my nostrils, twisting them, and my mouth burst open, spewing coins.

⌒

AS THE SAILORS gathered up the contraband and carried it away under Red's watchful eye, the swineherd snapped his umbrella shut and ordered us to dress.

"Maintain silence. Bundle up your belongings. Squat when you're done. Laggards will be placed in irons."

Everything was muddled, smeared with pitch, and in the scramble that followed, some hands turned as sticky with greed as tar. Many wrangled fiercely though silently over items, especially coins, but I made no effort to stop those who snatched what was mine. The doctor had dismissed—in addition to the morose graybeard, the skeletal addict beside me, and a fellow with badly ulcerated feet—three who coughed, and had I feigned Ba's deep gurgling instead of attempting to hide my coins, I might have been making my first steps home. Sick with regret, it was all I could do to pick up a pair of tattered pants and sandals nobody else had claimed, pull them on, squat.

Looping a tagged cord around each of our necks, the swineherd instructed, "On board, you will be known by the number on your tag. This number matches the one painted on your berth."

The characters on mine looked like seven-hundred-and-seventy-nine. But they couldn't be. The devil-ship, although huge, had neither the length nor the breadth of Strongworm, so how could it house more than twice the people in our village?

I peered again at the faded ink on my bamboo tag.

"No!"

Startled at hearing Small Eyes bellow, I looked up. He was nowhere in sight, and the swineherd was disappearing down the ladder while the devils who'd been posted at the ship's sides were closing in on us with their muskets raised.

At the advancing bayonets, captives—obviously as bewildered as myself—fell back on their heels, their bums. A few rose uncertainly. Moments later, prompted by the bayonets' sharp pricks, we were all on our feet, tumbling down the ladder, staggering over piles of tangled ropes, hurtling through a hatchway and down another ladder into a stinking, thundering darkness.

Rough hands shoved me forward. My sandaled feet sank into something sodden yet prickly; my nostrils tingled as if I were walking into a cloud of dust. The captives ahead were coughing and sneezing. Soon I was, too.

Shielding my nose with both hands, my elbows scraped wood. Were we in a walled passage? No, a narrow walkway between double-tiers of men, all shouting.

In the agitated jumble, I made out:

"Is the mandarin back?"

"Did he bring braves?"

A mandarin? Here? Small Eyes *had* sounded more anguished than bold. Was that why the swineherd had run, why the devils had abruptly driven us below?

As hope flickered, a stick rapped wood, punctuating, "Get into a berth. Never mind numbers for now. Any of these upper berths will do."

I was still unable to see much more than shadows, but from the scuffing and grunting on either side, I knew men were hoisting themselves up. Reaching out, I fumbled at a board level with my chest.

A knee, perhaps a heel, swiped my chin, and I jerked back, kicking metal. Liquid splashed my pants, soaked through to my calf, and the sharp odor of piss penetrated the general stink, setting off a string of curses.

The stick smashed my shoulder blades, knocking me flat against the board in a burst of pain.

"Up!"

Gripping the wood as though it were my tormentor's throat, I lifted myself, slamming my crown into the ceiling. My head ringing, I ducked, canted over the board, and scrambled into the berth, arousing more curses from those I pinched and kicked while wriggling into place.

⌒

THE BERTHS HAD no partitions, and my nose itched from the coiled queue of a lad whose back curved into my chest. My bum pressed into the softness of a fatty whose sour breath added to the curdled soup of odors from bilge, waste, unwashed men.

Water slapped the hull, making it even harder for me to distinguish individual words from the clamor. Hoping to confirm we were about to be rescued, I strained to catch snippets of talk in the two dialects I understood, to string these snippets into some sort of order.

The devil-ship had been loading captives for a month.

The stick wielder who'd driven us into our berths was a "corporal." Corporals, one for every fifty of us, were captives too, chosen by the swineherd for their muscle, their willingness to enforce order for the devils who did not come below if they could avoid it.

A few days ago, a couple of dozen armed devils stormed down the ladder into the two walkways separating the three tiers of berths. The swineherd, hard on their heels, hissed into the shocked silence, "Move one muscle, say one word, make one sound, and you're dead."

In the unnatural quiet, the men in the berths became aware of an argument above decks. They recognized Red's voice, the twitchy interpreter's, but not the one speaking the formal Saang Wah of the gentry.

"I insist you show me the passenger list."

"The captain's ashore. I can't release it without his authority."

"I have here a petition from the relatives of seven kidnapped men, and I will not leave this vessel until I've examined your passenger list for their names."

Back and forth they went. Finally, Red submitted to the stranger's demand. And when the stranger declared a match for three names, Red sent Twitchy to fetch them.

In the between-decks, the devils had their swords, the muzzles of their muskets, the points of their bayonets inches from the men in their berths. So although the lucky three had heard the stranger say their numbers, they did not dare leave until the swineherd gave them permission.

After they followed Twitchy above, there was knocking on the deck, probably the lucky three kowtowing, then their heartfelt thanks, an urgent plea on behalf of those still below because they, too, had been decoyed or kidnapped.

The stranger demanded a response from Red to the charge.

"The rest are willing passengers," Red protested through Twitchy. "I have their contracts to prove it."

The pleader among the lucky three countered that the contracts were bogus, that the men, like themselves, had either been tricked or forced into signing. He begged the stranger to go into the between-decks and question the captives.

Red blustered, Twitchy translated, "Mistakes happen. Keep your advance as compensation."

There was the clatter and roll of coins, the soft tread of cloth soles crossing planks. Those in the berths nearest the ladder, staring into the light, saw a mandarin in rich robes appear in the hatchway, recoil, thrust a large silk hankerchief to his nose. But the mandarin was looking into the dark. So he couldn't have seen them. He couldn't have known why no one left the between-decks after he called for those who were unwilling emigrants to go to him.

In any case, he was unlikely to have brought a force capable of subduing so many armed devils. That must be why the pleader did not then press him. Now the mandarin was back with soldiers to fight the devils and a fleet of junks that would carry us all to safety.

"Carry us to other devil-ships you mean."

"That's what happened to us."

"Believe me, unless your family is one of wealth and influence, you don't stand a chance in hell of returning home. Not now. Not ever."

Listening to the men wrangle, the flicker of hope in my chest flared bright, then waned: If we were just going to be delivered to another devil-ship, what difference did it make whether the mandarin had returned?

Into my mind came the picture of our captors marching us through the cobbled streets between the quay and the pigpen with no attempt to hide the fact that we were shackled. Of course, prisoners were routinely paraded. But on this devil-ship alone there were almost eight hundred captives. Since there were other devil-ships in the harbor, the number of shackled men marched through the streets must be in the thousands. Even a fool would have to wonder why there were so many criminals, why they were all being loaded onto foreign vessels. As for officials, they must be deliberately refusing to see, refusing to act except when their hands were forced. No wonder Young Master's father had managed to save him but Moongirl had lamented.

I groaned. The timbers against my head vibrated. From above came the prolonged rattle of chains, voices raised in unison. The rhythm was obviously that of a work song. Amidst the chanting I detected the grunts of men lifting a heavy weight, guessed the sailors were raising anchor, groaned again.

Around me, talk faded into moans, open weeping. Suddenly, the hull creaked, shuddered into motion. With nothing to hold onto, I'd have been thrown out of the berth were it not for the lip of wood at my feet.

Abruptly the ship lurched. The lad's head crashed into my nose. His elbows and knees jabbed. Mine scraped wood, sank into the fatty. There were cries, thuds, smelly clouds of straw and dirt churning up, coughing, sticks striking wood.

"Back in your berths!"

"That means you!"

"And you!"

"Now!"

Again the ship swung, pitching us into each other, the walkway. My cries, however, were not so much because of the ship's crazed lunges as for Bo See.

⌐

AS THE YOUNGEST daughter-in-law in our family, Bo See was expected to rise earlier than the rest of the household to fetch the day's water from the village well, then prepare

Ba's orange-rind brew, Ma's tea, and a basin of hot water for their morning wash. But I always rose with Bo See, and while she split kindling and started a fire in the kitchen stove, I'd set off at a trot to fill our waterbuckets.

Of course I was laughed at for doing women's work. I didn't care: My help allowed Bo See and I to linger in bed together until the square of sky in the window was tinged a faint pink. Now Bo See was alone in our bed, rising in the dark, stepping out of the house before cockcrow.

The street would be lively with other women on the same errand. At the clackety-clack of Bo See's wooden clogs, their chatter would fall away. They wouldn't shut Bo See out completely. At least they never had. They just wouldn't include her in talk beyond an exchange of greetings, the kind of polite conversation that passes between strangers rather than close neighbors, friends.

Long ago, Bo See had confided with a rueful smile that she'd been similarly treated in her home village. "Not always. But after people realized from the bride price my parents demanded that our family's success in raising silkworms came from me rather than luck. Even my close friends shut me out."

Exceptional skills were bound to arouse jealousy. Where Bo See's family had insisted she keep her skills secret, though, Ma had said, "The way of Heaven is fairness. We can't harm others by refusing to share what you know."

So Bo See had searched the dark corners and rafters of every wormhouse in Strongworm for insects that might lay eggs on the family's worms or suck their blood. She'd instructed wives not to cook with ginger or beans and cautioned those in charge of the wormhouses to sniff each person who entered to make sure there was nothing odorous on their persons. She'd demonstrated how she slapped the dust from the hems of her pants before entering a wormhouse, how she further purified herself with sprinkles of water from a basin placed just inside the door for that purpose. She'd explained that in catering to the silkworms' sensitivity, it wasn't enough to entice them onto fresh paper with mulberry instead of flicking them with a brush or feather; it was important to speak softly, to be mindful of their feelings. "Silkworms can sense the least agitation, so you must be calm inside and out."

Still no family met with success like ours, and people blamed Bo See for hiding something important.

"No one is hiding anything," Ma protested over and over. "It's the calm Bo See has brought to our wormhouse that makes our success exceed yours."

"Calm?"

"Bo See?"

"We're not blind, you know."

"Or without memory."

"Yeah! I thought *I* was a nervous bride, but Bo See had me beat."

"Me, too."

"Even with her escort holding her up, Bo See was swaying like a reed in a big wind."

Our family explained that Bo See had been suffering from motion sickness, not nervousness. We pointed out that she'd performed every ritual perfectly despite her near faint. Surely that was proof of extraordinary self-control.

Then people held Bo See at a distance for being unnatural.

My HUSBAND AND his brothers often complained that silkworms were greedy as the worst landlords, delicate and temperamental as gentry.

Our sisters-in-law groused that silkworms were more trouble than babies. Not only did silkworms have to be fed constantly, but the mulberry had to be exactly right. If the leaves were too old or not yet mature or still wet with dew, the worms would sicken. If the knives used for shredding were dull, there'd be insufficient sap for nourishment. If the pieces weren't fine enough or too long, the worms would not eat them.

Certainly Ba had to carefully assess our mulberry every day. Whenever it looked like we might run short of mature leaves, he had to send Ah Lung and his brothers in all directions to find more. Ba also had to do whatever was necessary to pay for the leaves our worms required, whether it was hiring out my sisters-in-law to reel cocoons for the village landlords, pawning our winter quilts, borrowing against a future harvest, or telling Ma we'd have to make do with watery gruel instead of rice.

During the nine-month silk season, seven generations of silkworms, each numbering in the thousands, had to be raised, and every hand capable of labor, even a child's, had to help cultivate the mulberry, pick the leaves, shred them, feed the worms, clean their trays, place them on spinning racks, smother the chrysalids in their cocoons, reel the silk, begin again.

I'd started working when I was five, as had my brother. Where he'd quit the wormhouse for play as soon as he'd completed his tasks, however, I'd lingered in the silkworms' thrall.

Newly hatched, they were shorter than my smallest fingernail, black as my hair and as fine. Yet they'd know to rear up, sway from side to side in search of mulberry. As I sprinkled finely chopped leaves over them, they'd seize the slivers in their tiny jaws, and so loud was their collective crunching and grinding that it would muffle the chop-chop-chop of the cleavers preparing more mulberry.

Eating nonstop, the worms quickly doubled in size, swelled until they had to shed their skin or burst. But first they'd fall into an eerie quiet in which they slept with their little heads crooked skyward, gathering the strength necessary to make a new skin, wriggle out of the old.

Each of their four new skins was lighter in color than the last, and the worms would, after thirty-two days, become a luminous white-amber, long and thick as my mother's middle finger. Then they'd start spinning silk from their mouths, and through deft tilting and looping shroud themselves completely.

This silk was the harvest for which everyone toiled, and it fetched far more on the market after the strands had been reeled from the cocoons, wound into skeins. Whether reeling silk or picking mulberry leaves, however, I'd be impatient to return to the worms themselves. And while my parents and brother celebrated the end of a season, I'd be eagerly anticipating the next.

I still did. Indeed, during the three months our wormhouse stood silent, my sisters-in-law liked to joke that I paced and fidgeted like an addict deprived of her opium. When at last it thrummed with life again, my husband's brothers would ask him:

"Does Bo See take care of your worm this tenderly?"

"Is your worm neglected now that she has charge of thousands?"

Despite their teasing and grousing, my brothers- and sisters-in-law always placed the well-being of the worms before their own, and they taught their children to do the same. Without exception, then, every member of the family old enough to work labored as diligently as I did to ensure our worms' contentment. For they understood that the less satisfied our worms, the poorer their appetites and the quality of their cocoons, hence the family's profit. Moreover, the moths that emerged and the eggs they laid would be inferior, affecting the family's income through several generations of worms. Should our worms, weakened from eating too little, sicken and perish, so would the family.

Fourth Brother-in-law, in doubling the family's worry and leaving us short of his hands as well as Ah Lung's, clearly had not followed his own teaching when catching a fastboat for Canton. Had I thought for a moment that my presence would contribute to my husband's rescue, though, I would have jumped into a boat, too.

~⸙

AFTER FOURTH BROTHER-IN-LAW'S arrival in Canton, Moongirl, through the husband of a patron, secured the help of a mandarin in finding mine.

This mandarin—forbidding and stiff as his black lacquered hat and high-collared, brocaded robe—had lost his only son to pig-traders, and he'd since executed all kidnappers caught within his jurisdiction no matter how heavily their families or associates weighted pleas for mercy with silver ingots, how much the wretches themselves soaked the earth with their tears. He also committed his personal wealth as well as the resources of his office to looking for stolen men.

Promising to scour the vicinity and outlying areas for Ah Lung, the mandarin counseled Moongirl and Fourth Brother-in-law to extend their search beyond his authority to Macao, the loading point for devil-ships. He provided them with letters of introduction to appropriate officials; passage on a speedy fire-driven boat; even the protection of a barrel-chested lieutenant armed with a sharp-edged broadsword.

The captains and crews of riverboats were sometimes overcome by man-stealers posing as passengers or in attacks launched from vessels alongside. So braves armed with muskets patrolled the deck of the fire-driven boat, and the lieutenant's sword-hand never shifted from his weapon's hilt.

His other hand waving off fiery-hot cinders and throat-searing billows of smoke, the lieutenant grimly jutted out his chin, directing Moongirl's and Fourth Brother-in-law's attention to the rotting hulks, secluded bays, and grassy islands that were once the refuge of opium smugglers, now pig-traders; the stone forts—embowered by shady banyans, flowering acacias, and dense bamboo groves—from which soldiers hunted them down.

The lieutenant hawked his disgust, spit over the railing. "Evil-doers are like autumn leaves. No sooner are some swept away, then more take their place."

To Moongirl, the river—muddy with silt—smelled as much of earth as water, and as the fire-boat chugged past junks and sampans, the deck pulsed beneath her feet like a live animal, reminding her of the buffalo she and Ah Lung had ridden as children, the games of hide-and-go-seek they'd played.

Suddenly he felt very close, and she wondered out loud whether Ah Lung might be hidden beneath an awning or in the hold of a nearby boat.

The lieutenant dismissed the possibility. "More likely your brother's already in a pigpen or devil-ship."

"What are his chances of escape?"

"From a pigpen? Next to none. Not in one piece anyway. Same for a devil-ship so long as it's at anchor in the harbor. There are too many guards. But captives on most ships organize rebellions soon after they're at sea, and although few of these mutinies succeed, some of the rebels do escape."

Making a fist, the lieutenant rapped his barrel-chest, then his forehead.

"What's required is courage and good planning."

~~~~

EVEN AS THE fire-driven boat was tying up at the quay, Moongirl was leaning over the railing, hiring a skiff. Then, while Fourth Brother-in-law and the lieutenant hurried off to deliver the mandarin's letters to officials and urge thorough searches of pigpens, lists of men already boarded, Moongirl leaped onto the skiff and directed the boatman to nose out devil-ships in the crowded harbor.

She knew from the lieutenant that devil-ships could be identified by their smell. But so terrible was their stink that were it not for the drone of talk from the holds, Moongirl would have thought the ships filled with captured beasts.

Yet Moongirl refused the boatman's offer of a cloth to cover her nose and mouth as he circled the devil-ships. There was such a din from bird cries, men bawling and swearing, that she was afraid her voice, if the least bit muffled, would fail to penetrate the thick planks of the ships' hulls.

Nor did Moongirl shout, "Ah Lung," the way men and women on other skiffs were calling the names of brothers, husbands, sons, and fathers. She chanted the lament, "Savages have taken you prisoner," in hopes that Ah Lung, should he hear her, would heed its warning.

She never expected to see him. And since she was partially blinded by a fierce glare, Moongirl couldn't be sure the man mounting a narrow gangplank stretched between junk and devil-ship actually *was* Ah Lung. With soldiers on both sides of the gangplank aiming their muskets at him though, Moongirl realized that whether she startled the man and he fell or he responded to her by deliberately jumping, he'd be shot. So she did not cry, "Ah Lung," even then. Instead she promised the boatman, "Double pay for doubling your pace," and raced to shore for an official.

BACK AGAIN ON the devil-ship's gangplank, I was walking towards Moongirl and freedom when I misstepped, fell. At the rush of air, my arms flew up, my jacket ballooned out, floated over my mouth and nose.

Reminding myself that I was holding my breath, I did nothing foolish. Not even when the force with which I hit water stung my feet, ripped loose my pants.

Once submerged, my pants torqued around my legs; the jacket's grip on my head tightened. In a flash, I was shackled and shrouded, and I clawed and kicked in a panic.

For what seemed forever, the water churned as wildly as myself. Then Bo See's arms were encircling me and all turned calm.

Little by little, though, disparate sensations pricked this calm:

The distant chimes of a bell.

Curses, mutterings, harsh heaving.

More chimes, closer and clearer; a shout.

Fetid heat, flesh—not Bo See's—sticking to mine.

The slap of bare feet, clank of buckets and pump.

My mouth filling with water, the taste of salt.

A wracking wet cough that brought back full awareness—and with it, the bitter knowledge that Moongirl had not returned and I was yet a captive on the devil-ship, squeezed between Ah Jook on my left, Ah Ming on my right.

⌐

THE OFFICIAL FOUND my husband's name in a list of eight-hundred captives on board a devil-ship headed for Peru, a country even further away than Gold Mountain on the other side of the world. So the man Moongirl saw on the gangplank probably *had* been Ah Lung. And although the devil-ship had sailed before he could be rescued, Fourth Brother-in-law reminded the family, "There's still a chance Ah Lung will return home through a mutiny. A good chance. That's why Moongirl didn't come back with me. She's expecting Ah Lung to land in Canton any day."

I WAS CONFUSED by the frequent ringing of bells on the devil-ship until Ah Ming—who'd lived in America—explained they were for marking time: "We divide our days into twelve hours, but foreigners on land divide theirs into two cycles of twelve, at sea into six cycles, each beginning with one bell and ending with eight. So every half-hour, the helmsman is responsible for striking a small bell behind him. Then a sailor strikes a larger bell. But it's the watch who calls out the number of chimes and 'All's well.'"

Every morning, at four bells during the second cycle, the sailors on the devil-ship started scrubbing the decks. Soon water would drip down on us through the seams in the planking. Since the hull leaked as well, we were never dry. Neither were our berths. Yet we were forced to remain in them except when compelled by necessity to use the wastebuckets located at the stern of the between-decks.

With only eight buckets for close to eight hundred men, many of whom were suffering motion sickness, the wait was always long, the crush in the walkways terrible, and those unable to hold in their vomit or piss or shit would aim for the nearest spittoon. Not surprisingly, spittoons *and* buckets overflowed long before their removal, spilled as they were carried out.

Ah Jook, a ship's carpenter in Hong Kong before his capture, claimed the large pipes near the buckets were to draw off foul air. To me, though, these pipes seemed as ineffectual as the three heavily grated hatches which let in little light, less air, not the faintest whiff of a breeze.

When in our berths, I could barely make out Ah Jook's thick neck and bunlike cheeks, the giant mole—black and hairy—between Ah Ming's eyebrows, the oversized teeth crowded behind his thin, colorless lips. I could only tolerate the stink by breathing through my mouth, counting each ding of the bells until the four in the third and fifth cycles signaled our morning and afternoon meals.

It was not the food I wanted. Because of the stink, the ship's roll that endlessly pushed my soles flat against the lip of wood at my feet then shoved my head against the hull, the state of my stomach ricocheted from queasiness to outright rebellion. But one of every ten captives had to fetch the food from above for the other nine, and I'd seized this job of "steward" so I could stretch my limbs and breathe fresh air twice a day.

Anticipating four bells, I'd hoist my legs over the platform's lip at the first ding. Although I tried to be careful,
my queue—long enough for me to sit on—would usually
uncoil from around the crown of my head, become entan-
gled in the awkward convolutions of my limbs. I'd arouse
grumbles, curses from Ah Ming and Ah Jook and those in
the crowded walkway whose ears, chins, chests, bums, or
knees I poked and kicked.

Long before I landed, I'd feel my feet and calves prick-
le. Still I'd have to stamp the sodden straw in the walkway
to bring my legs fully to life, and since there was no way to
hurry through the men choking the narrow passage, I'd
always find stewards ahead of me at the ladder.

From painful experience, I knew the grating in the
hatch was blistering hot, and when my turn came to
mount the ladder, I'd blink my eyes to adjust them to the
dazzling light above, pause on the last tread to make sure
of my balance, my ability to safely negotiate the opening.
Finally, I'd step past the pair of armed devils guarding the
hatch and eagerly gulp untainted air to cleanse my mouth,
my throat, then breathe deeply through my nose.

The cookhouse—midway between the hatch and the
foremast—was no more than ten or twelve paces away.
Even so, stick-wielding corporals hemmed us in on both
sides. When Ah Choy, a steward from my home district,
asked me to take part in a mutiny by smuggling a knife
from the cookhouse into the between-decks, however, my

heart did not quail for fear of the corporals' sticks or the devils' muskets, bayonets, swords, and shackles, but their lash.

⌒

RULES FOR THE between-decks were posted under all three hatches, and topping the list of "crimes punishable with the lash" was gambling. Yet the man-stealers had knowingly decoyed gamblers, and the thieves in the pig-pen had encouraged purchases of dice, paper cards, bamboo dominoes, and checkers to wile away the time at sea in play. Is it any wonder our quarters were as infested with gamblers as bugs? Some were even gaming with the pests.

Old Eight in the berth directly opposite mine would flip two cockroaches onto their backs, pin them into the wood, side by side, and then drop a little piece of straw on top of each. The roaches—instinctively, I suppose— would grasp and pass the straw from one pair of their legs to the other, over and over, and Old Eight would take wagers on which would be the first to collapse in exhaustion.

Also gambling with cockroaches were Toothless and Big Belly. Except they tickled their roaches with straw, irri-tating them the way boys and gamblers back home did crickets, until the creatures fought.

The cockroaches kept fighting after they were injured. They'd struggle to keep moving the straw back and forth long after their legs' initial frantic churning slowed to a drag. Did they somehow realize that once they gave up, they'd be squashed dead and replaced?

To make room for their roaches, Old Eight, Toothless, and Big Belly had to dangle their feet over the edges of their berths. Gamblers using dominoes or checkers, which required more space, had to sit with their knees drawn up to their chins, their backs hunched, their heads bowed.

Since the height of the between-decks from floor to ceiling was barely five-and-a-half feet and our berths were double-tiered, we were compelled to eat our meals like this. A bowl of rice, though, was finished in a matter of moments while a game could stretch from the chiming of one bell to another—and another.

I'd pass gamblers thus huddled whenever I was in the walkway, and while waiting to use a wastebucket, I was sometimes invited to join in. Even if I'd had money, I'd have refused. But I gave the players my full attention. As children, Moongirl, our friends, and I had often played the game in which a fist represents a stone, an outstretched hand water, and curved fingers a bowl. I'd had fun whether my bowl managed to capture someone else's water or their water swept away my stone instead of my stone breaking another player's bowl. So I'd never tried to anticipate my opponents' strategies or made any of my own. I'd never trained myself to make accurate judgments, decisions, and changes in haste the way Moongirl had urged me to, the way she did. Realizing that this failing was, at least in part, why I'd been bested repeatedly by my captors, I was attempting to change by studying them, my fellow captives, especially the gamblers and corporals.

The corporals, I noted, received a hefty percentage of the money passing through the gamblers' hands. Similarly, the corporals accepted bribes to overlook theft and fighting, which were also punishable with the lash.

When Ah Bun—three berths down from me—broke the rule which prohibited smoking in the between-decks though, the corporals jeered at him for offering them cash to spare him.

"Wah, you really are bun, stupid."

"Straw burns, you idiot. Wood, too."

"What good is your cash if we burn to death?"

"Have mercy," Ah Bun pleaded. "I didn't think."

"You got that right!"

"Now you won't forget."

Nor would any of us who witnessed Ah Bun's suffering after the corporals returned him to his berth. And where Ah Bun had suffered the twelve strokes prescribed for smokers, gamblers, fighters, and thieves, the punishment for mutiny was forty-eight lashes, after which the mutineer would be chained to the ringbolts of the stern deck until released by the captain.

From the glimpses I'd caught of him, the captain seemed almost mousy he was so small and gray. But no mouse would have charge of a devil-ship let alone permit the use of a whip that had nine separate cords, each weighted with jagged slatherings of tar.

Ah Bun, in a voice faint from screaming, told us the sensation of those nine sharply-edged cords simultaneously flaying open his flesh was like that of molten lead. "By the second stroke, I was praying I'd die. After the fourth, I passed out. The devils revived me before going on. Not just that once. Every time."

RUMOR HAD IT that the captain, furious because the doctor's dismissals would short him six captives, had abducted Small Eyes. Then, when the swineherd had rushed to defend Small Eyes, the captain had accused them both of fraud. In the ruckus that had followed, the swineherd and Small Eyes had somehow managed to leap overboard, and the crew from the junk had saved them. Otherwise, the two would have been whipped and chained alongside the pointy-eared resister I'd seen shackled to the stern deck when I'd first boarded.

Whether this resister was still in irons, I was uncertain. He had not been brought below. Neither had he been seen in the sickroom located directly behind the main mast. Sleepy checked whenever he went for what Twitchy, translating for the doctor, called "a dose of medicinal opium." I'd also try to look while fetching our meals from the cookhouse. But all I could see of the sickroom was the area outside where Sleepy and others with the opium habit stretched out to take their dose, and my view of the stern deck was blocked by the sails billowing from the main mast, the buffalo tethered beneath the ship's longboat, which was piled high with caged hens and pigs.

There was little meat in our rice. Yet every day there were sounds of slaughter, and I'd seen the knives and cleavers necessary for butchering in the cookhouse. Was it really possible that, as instructed by Ah Choy, I need only scratch my left ear while waiting for tomorrow's morning meal, and a cook would hide one in my basket?

That the cooks—Pockface, Shorty, and Ah Kow—were willing to participate in a mutiny, perhaps even lead it, rang true. Pockface, a butcher in Canton, had been kidnapped on his way to visit his parents in their home village; Shorty and Ah Kow, cooks at a large restaurant in the city, had been decoyed by an acquaintance who'd told them there were openings with better wages in a Macao gambling house, and the three ranted about their captivity. So did Ah Choy.

But the cooks' helpers, Big Buffalo and Little Buffalo, wore greasy smiles. Before voluntarily signing contracts for labor overseas, both men had been unemployed porters who ate only when they were lucky enough to find a grave with offerings of food they could steal. Now their mouths were never empty. Indeed, it was their continuous grazing in the cookhouse that had earned them their nicknames.

I was certain they wouldn't mutiny, and there were bound to be others, especially among the corporals, opium eaters, and gamblers—those who found the risk of injury and death worse than a future in captivity without family. In the shipyard where Ah Jook had labored though, much of the work had been the conversion of foreign vessels for the more profitable trade in men, and he said the number of crew on a devil-ship this size was about fifty. Say just half the captives mutineed, we'd still outnumber the devils eight to one. Moreover, there were former soldiers among us.

True, Red and the sailors had confiscated anything they found that could be turned into a weapon. Despite the thoroughness of their searches, however, they'd failed to discover some items. How else would Old Eight have pins to hold his cockroaches in place? Pins that could be made into weapons. And although every sailor seemed to have a knife hanging from a strap about his waist, the knives in the cookhouse—many times larger and made for cutting flesh—were sure to be more effective in battle. Even against muskets. At least the way the devils had used their muskets when captives had rushed the hatches shortly after sailing.

Pinned in my berth by the ship's wild bucking, I hadn't realized what was happening. But above the awful rending of the ship's timbers, the whacks of the corporals' sticks, their shouted commands, I'd been aware of a solid, desperate roar that was shattered by a series of small explosions, the distinctive smell of gunpowder, shrieks of terror and pain.

Later, I learned the devils had fired their muskets directly at the captives clawing the hatch gratings from below. Those shot had fallen onto the men beneath them. They in turn, had tumbled onto others. Then, as the fallen had piled up, the ship's crazed pitching and lurching had shaken them loose, hurling bodies into the men choking the walkways, the corporals crushed among them, toppling all.

In the flailing muddle, the efforts to disentangle sticks and limbs, many had suffered severe grazes and bruising, a few broken bones. But those of us who'd remained in our berths bore similar injuries from the ship's lunges and rolls. As for the men shot by the devils' muskets, none died. Their wounds were mere blazes of purpled skin. For the devils had fired pellets of seasalt, and I expected they'd do likewise when fighting mutineers. Not out of mercy. No. But because we were the captain's goods.

⁓

ACCORDING TO AH Jook, the captains of devil-ships protected the wheelhouses on their vessels with iron barricades, and the one we'd passed through when herded onto the stern deck for inspection was typical: About eight feet high and stretching from bulwark to bulwark, it had a single gate flanked by two openings for a pair of cannons that were positioned to rake the ship's main deck. My eyes fixed on the devils and their weapons, I'd failed to see either the cannons or the barricade. Did the leaders of the mutiny know about them? Was overcoming cannons and a barricade in their plan?

Even with the cannons shooting pellets of seasalt, I doubted the barricade could be breached unless the devils were taken by surprise—and by a large force. Which meant it had to be stormed at the very start of the mutiny.

Red or some other devil surely counted the knives in the cookhouse before Shorty, Pockface, Ah Kow, and the two Buffalos returned to their berths for the night. The mutiny, then, would have to begin in the afternoon. The three cooks wouldn't be foolish enough to fight alone or to rely on immediate help from below. Could there be mutineers among the men going above for opium?

Those without cash were allowed to charge the cost of the opium against future earnings, and I'd heard more than a few who went for "medicinal doses" make fun of the doctor for failing to recognize that they didn't have the habit. But I'd thought I knew why they were going. While in line for our meals or washing our bowls and chopsticks, I'd watched many a man collect his tiny jar of opium, stretch on a mat, take out a speck at the end of a wire, carefully warm it over the flame of a lamp, press it into the porcelain bowl of his pipe, then dip in for more. Back and forth he'd go, heating the opium, working it into the proper sticky consistency. Finally, the man would suck on the pipe's stem, and although family teaching had instilled in me that pipedreams were both fleeting and false, I'd wish my own head was filling with hot, sweet smoke, bringing dreams of happiness with Bo See.

Returning home through a mutiny might be a pipedream, too. With no other chance for escape though, I'd accepted Ah Choy's invitation to join. Now I prayed to Gwan Gung—the heavily bearded, red-faced God of War who champions right as much as might—for another Sahm Yuen Lei.

DURING THE FIRST war over opium, a devil-general had landed five thousand English and Indian troops north of Canton. Our soldiers, taken by surprise, had been overwhelmed, and the devil-soldiers had easily captured the five forts that protected the city's north gate.

Heaping injury upon injury, this devil-general ordered cannons set up where they disturbed the fung sui, the natural order of wind and water, for the villages in the area. He sent devil-soldiers into the countryside to forage for food.

Some of these devil-soldiers not only stole livestock but willfully trampled crops, looted villas, plundered temples, opened graves, and molested defenseless women. Cowed by the devils' guns, none of the abused fought back— until a night patrol forced its way into a home just outside Sahm Yuen Lei and the screams from the household's women so outraged the men in the village that they overcame their fears and rushed to the rescue.

These men drove out the devil-soldiers with their bare fists! Then, emboldened by their success, the men of Sahm Yuen Lei beat on drums and gongs, rallying others to push the devil-general and his troops back into the sea.

Almost eight thousand men from over one hundred villages responded. The villagers had nothing for weapons except their mattocks and hoes. But their rage made them brave, and they advanced against the heavily armed devils, attacking with such vigor that they broke the enemy's ranks. Soon after, Gwan Gung splintered the sky with loud volleys of thunder and lightning, letting loose rain that disabled the devils' guns, and the villagers won a great victory.

As word of my husband's capture and his brother's pursuit spread through Strongworm, people shrilled alarm and wild speculation. The very air began to crackle and throb. Worry felled Ma, then Ba, leaving Eldest Sister and Brother-in-law in charge.

The family, unlike the village, had always heeded my call for absolute calm when around worms. Only Moongirl, however, had ever managed to shed her feelings in the wormhouse the way I did. On those occasions when strong emotions had rocked other family members, they'd restricted themselves to outside work.

Now Fourth Sister-in-law, her eyes red-rimmed and puffy, prepared medicines and meals. Together with Eldest Sister-in-law, she nursed Ma and Ba, directed Eldest Niece in the care of the children too young to work.

Snatching time from reeling cocoons, Second and Third Sisters-in-law helped their husbands hang heavy winter quilts over the ceiling beam in the middle of the family's main room in order to contain cooking odors that wafted in from the kitchen, smoke and fragrance from the altar's candles and incense. They also cleared the furniture and clutter from the side that was smoke- and odor-free, scrubbed its walls and floor clean of soot and grit, installed the chopping blocks and knives from the wormhouse.

Then, while Second and Third Sisters-in-law returned to reeling, my brothers-in-law and their children picked mulberry. Every day they brought in fresh leaves from the fields and prepared them for our worms. They packed the chopped leaves in baskets, then carried them the twenty, twenty-five steps to the door of our wormhouse, a small brick outbuilding on the other side of our courtyard wall.

Each of the freestanding shelves within held a half-dozen trays of worms, and I alone had to feed all. Nevertheless, I took the time to carefully distribute the leaves in an even layer above their pointed mouths so no worm would injure another by crawling over it in order to eat. As they grew, I increased the size of the trays to prevent overcrowding, thus reducing the danger of any being squashed or suffocated. When they soiled their trays' paper linings, I gave them fresh.

Of course, one pair of hands, even working ceaselessly, could not possibly feed thousands of hungry worms fast enough, and although Eldest Sister-in-law had excused me from household tasks, I'd have to leave from time to time to use the privy, wash, change my clothes, down a mouthful of rice, or sink onto a bedmat between the shelves to snatch a moment of sleep.

Despite my best efforts to keep up, some worms became impatient while waiting for fresh mulberry. Straining for the tough, inedible scraps that collected at the bottom of trays, they crushed those in their path.

The count of dead was low, however, and the worms' lusty appetites proved their good health, the family's effectiveness in shielding them from our troubles.

Every morning, directly after four bells, a pair of corporals escorted the cooks and their helpers to the cookhouse. Wedged between my berthmates, I couldn't see them. But the noise in the between-decks at that hour was sufficiently muted that I could hear the corporals rapping their sticks against one berth, then another.

"Aaargh," someone croaked. "Can't you poke them awake?"

"Poke yourself," Pockface snapped. "Better yet, go cook so I can have a lie in."

"Ai," Little Buffalo whimpered.

"Get your ass down here," Corporal Woo ordered.

"I'm sick," Little Buffalo whined.

Big Buffalo groaned. "Me, too."

Shorty snorted. "Lazy more like."

"Greedy," Ah Kow said above the sound of retching. "I warned those two the meat was rotten."

"What meat?" Corporal Woo demanded.

"Scraps from the devils' garbage."

"That's enough talk." Corporal Woo rapped his stick impatiently. "Let's go."

There were curses, calls for them to hurry up about it, protests from Pockface, Ah Kow, and Shorty that they couldn't cook for eight hundred without help.

"Three-three-three," Corporal Lee shouted. "To the cookhouse!"

"Not yet," Ah Choy groused. "I'm a steward."

"You're what I say you are," Corporal Lee came back. "You, too, three-three-four."

"Pick someone else," Warts told him.

Stick smacked flesh.

"Alright, alright," Warts cried. "I'm coming."

Other mornings I'd distracted myself from my misery by tracking their departure: the muffled footfalls; the faint clicks of latches for the removal of the two night lanterns from their cages at either end of the between-decks; the rasp and clang as the devils unlocked the gate in the hatch and threw it open. Today, sailors were already clattering about the deck, scrubbing the planks. Men directly below them were thumping the ceiling with their fists, cursing the water splashing through the cracks. I was silently thanking the God of Luck for the mutiny's auspicious start.

SHUFFLING FROM THE hatch to the cookhouse, I wondered whether Warts and Corporal Lee were part of the mutiny. I fretted that although the two Buffalos were gone, one of the corporals hemming us in might notice the knives in the cookhouse were disappearing into baskets of food and alert the devils. Or, since everybody in the between-decks itched from bugs embedded in the seams of clothes and nests of hair, a cook might mistake an ordinary scratch for the prearranged signal. Or, by ill fortune, Red or the captain or some other devil might walk past and catch a cook slipping a knife into a basket.

Questioned under the lash, anyone might endanger the mutiny. Reasoning I could tell the devils nothing if I knew nothing, I'd deliberately not asked Ah Choy any questions. Now I agonized over what I was supposed to do with the knife, how I could hide it before I set the basket in front of the men waiting for their morning rice.

Too late, I wished I'd taken Ah Jook or Ah Ming into my confidence and sought their help. I considered slipping the knife under Scholar Mok. One of the nine for whom I was steward, Scholar Mok had been kidnapped on his way to a literary exam, and he'd been deliberately courting death by refusing to eat or drink. In the past two days, he'd not left his berth. . . .

Knuckles in the small of my back pushed me forward, and a stick that would otherwise have landed on my shoulder whistled past.

"Keep the line moving!" the stick-wielding corporal barked.

Madly scratching my left ear, I stepped in front of Shorty, who handed me a pot of hot tea, a basket loaded with two stacks of bowls, a bundle of chopsticks, and a mound of rice flecked with bits of saltfish I might have missed but for their spicy fragrance. If the knife was under the rice, digging it out would be a mess. I eyed the bowls, which were laid on their sides.

"Looking for gold?" a corporal mocked.

"No, more of the devils' meat," Pockface joked.

The cooks, corporals, and stewards laughed. Horrified I was calling attention to myself, I slunk back to the hatch, matching my stride to the roll of the ship so as to maintain my balance.

Carefully I eased myself and the basket through the narrow opening in the grating, made my descent from sunlight into darkness, squeezed into the blur of darker shadows jamming the walkway.

Feet stomped mine. As I attempted to pull free without upsetting the basket, hot tea streamed from the pot I was clutching by the handle.

"Wai!"

"Look out!"

Hands grabbed the basket. I clung on. The bowls and chopsticks rattled.

The hands on the basket tugged harder. "Let me help you."

"It's not necessary," I insisted although the pot was swinging wildly, spilling more tea.

"Clumsy clot! You need all the help you can get."

"Really, I can manage."

"Alright, suit yourself."

So abruptly were the basket and my feet released that I tottered. Steadying myself, the basket felt lighter. I did, too.

AS USUAL I set the pot, then the basket, in my berth before climbing up, and all nine of us downed our rice swiftly and in silence. How could it be otherwise when we had our legs folded against our chests, our chins bumping our knees, and our shoulders, arms, elbows, and chopsticks chafing and jabbing one another? Moreover, our throats were always parched, so we were eager to empty our bowls for tea. Now, lifting just the pot, I understood in a flash that my load had lightened on account of the tea that had spilled. Had there even been a knife in the basket?

My hands shaking, I began to pour. With Scholar Mok's allotment added to ours, I'd previously been able to fill our bowls. Trying to stretch what was in the pot, I stopped far short of the rims, and I left my own bowl empty, stammering that I'd go without since I was at fault for spilling the tea on my way down.

"Swigging from the spout, you mean."

"Yeah, you've had your fill."

"And at our expense."

"You sneaky bastard."

"No wonder you pounced on the job of steward."

At the accusations, my throat closed, I could not utter a word of protest. Nor did anyone else defend me.

Suddenly, Ah Ming seized my bowl. The snarling over the missing tea stopped. Greedy Cat, a chubby youth kidnapped after he'd slipped away from friends to buy a snack, buried his face in his bowl.

His thin lips twisted in a grimace, Ah Ming poured a dollop of tea from his bowl into mine. Big Belly and Toothless cackled their scorn.

Ah Jook, shamefaced, mumbled, "I can't."

My voice rough from emotion and thirst, I urged, "Drink. Everybody. Drink."

Big Belly raised his bowl to his lips. "Damned right!"

Moaning, "My throat's sore as my back or I'd give you some," Ah Bun did likewise.

"Sure you would," Toothless sneered between gulps.

With the men around me sipping and slurping, my thirst worsened. But I offered to return the tea in my bowl to Ah Ming.

"Save your spit."

Hurt, I shrank into myself, not even daring to say thanks.

~

AH MING'S GIFT, gone in a single swallow, acted like a tease, and as I went above to wash up, I prayed the rain that had brought the victory at Sahm Yuen Lei would begin now.

It didn't seem much to ask since big winds at home brought heavy rains, and the wind whistling through the devil-ship's rigging was powerful, filling sails larger than our family's biggest fields. Above the deck where I squatted in front of the washbucket, however, the sky remained a torrid blaze of gold unmarked by clouds.

Desperate for relief, I plunged my hands past the bowls and chopsticks in the bucket of saltwater, splashing my face, my neck, my chest. The droplets cooled, but only for a moment. Then they vanished, leaving me hotter than ever. So I splashed myself again.

"This way, brother." The steward at the bucket nearest mine scooped water into two bowls, tipped them over his head.

The corporals encircling us growled.

"Stop that foolishness."

"Break a bowl and I'll break your head."

From inside the cookhouse came angry shouts.

"Quit bossing me!"

"I *am* your boss."

"*Dead* boss!"

"You threatening me?"

At the first shout, Corporal Lee had darted from the wash area. Since the cookhouse door was around the corner, we couldn't see him, but his calls for help were distinct, and several corporals left at a run.

Corporal Woo drummed his stick against the planks at his feet, bellowing, "Dah! Dah! Dah! Strike! Strike! Strike!"

My heart jumped. Was this the signal to mutiny? Or was Corporal Woo announcing trouble, calling for reinforcements from below?

Quickly, I twisted my head and flicked my eyes in search of clues. Corporals *and* stewards were gaping at Woo in stunned silence. The devil-sentries at the hatch had quit their posts and were aiming their muskets at us.

Yelling, "Duck!" I grasped the sides of my washbucket and hefted it up for a shield, soaking my pants, sending bowls and chopsticks crashing onto the deck.

Other stewards turning over their buckets added to the wetness and litter. Corporals dashing for cover cursed as they skidded on slick planks and scattered chopsticks, stumbled over unbroken bowls, fell, cut themselves on sharp-edged shards.

A musket fired. Another. At the blasts, the rat-a-tat on our makeshift shields, men screamed, and the acrid whiffs of gunpowder were soon smothered in the rank odor of bowels loosed by fear.

———

I NOW KNOW the cookhouse brawl was a trick to draw the corporals and devil-sentries from their posts. Moreover, while the cooks and their helpers cudgeled corporals they deemed untrustworthy, gagged and bound them, corporals committed to the mutiny converted their sticks into more lethal weapons by fitting the ends with well-honed blades, then ran forward to ferret out and subdue devils.

At the same time, mutineers below—alerted by Corporal Woo's signal that the hatchway was unguarded—led captives up the ladder and herded them towards the ship's stern, shouting, "Kill the devils! Take over the ship!" in multiple dialects. Some of the leaders snatched grappling hooks or chains, even the large, club-like pegs used to hold coiled rope along the ship's rail. Others attacked the devil-sentries, seized their muskets and fired them at the devils loading the cannons.

Flat on my belly behind my bucket-shield, I assumed the sentries were still shooting at us. Yet there was no rat-a-tat against wood.

Boom! The explosion shattered glass, my skull. The ship convulsed, threatened to break. Men shrieked and wailed. Perhaps I did, too.

Boom! In the aftershock of this second blast, I rolled

helplessly on the pitching deck; my head and limbs slammed flesh, metal, wood; my skin prickled and burned. Amidst the cries of men and devils, pigs squealed, buffalos drummed their hooves, chickens squawked.

"Kill the devils! Take the ship!"

I slitted my eyes, which were watering, as was my nose. Caustic smoke was billowing over bodies, buckets, all manner of debris. A piece of firewood slithered within reach. Snagging it, I realized salt-pellets beaded the deck. So the devils *weren't* using lead! Emboldened, I sprang upright, but I misjudged the ship's roll and toppled onto my knees, the landing so jarring I felt impaled.

A musket discharged. Would a cannon be next? Doubling over, I covered my head with both arms, prayed the devils would stay with salt instead of lead and Gwan Gung would split open the cloudless sky, silencing the devils' weapons with rain.

"Kill the devils! Take the ship!"

Lowering my arms, I cautiously poked up my head, peered through the thin shreds of smoke the wind had yet to blow away. Captives were streaming out of the hatch. Most had not been on deck since boarding, and for many, as much as a month had passed, for some even more. Stiff-legged from their long confinement and doubtless blinded by the light and smoke, they soon stumbled and crashed. An instant later though, they were scrambling back to their feet, raising their fists to the sky, yelling, "Kill the devils! Take the ship!" Shamed, I added my voice to theirs and lurched towards the ragged charge.

Each man's stumble affected the rest and, more than once, I was toppled by someone reeling into me, sending others flying. Nor was I alone in hurling myself onto the deck at the sound of gunfire. Over and over, however, we picked ourselves up. Those without weapons scooped up suitable debris.

By the time we reached the main mast, the devils were using lead; many of us were stamping our feet as if we were soldiers marching into battle. Then, to avoid the danger-ous mess of raucous livestock to the left of the sickroom, we lunged to the right as one, and so tightly were we packed that no one could fall, not even the man whose head exploded like an overripe melon. Or those like myself who, splattered with skin and blood and bone, might also have felt their legs turn to water.

Our chant did falter, and at the frightening clash of metal, anguished cries, and murderous yowls that burst into the lull, it almost disappeared. To give myself heart, I again bawled, "Kill the devils! Take the ship!" Other men did, too. Roaring, we spilled into the area directly in front of the iron barricade.

The headless man sagged onto the planks and slid on the canted deck, tripping those in his path. Muskets fired. A few in the lead fell, flattening more. But most of us kept marching, and our feet pounded loud and strong.

Through fleeting gaps, I saw the barricade had been breached despite the menacing spikes topping its thick rails. I couldn't make out anything more than flashes of swords, axes, and cleavers, but the crush of devils and men locked in battle seemed to make reloading the cannons impossible and the fighting at the gate looked especially fierce, with men madly slashing and hacking while devils endeavored to force it shut against our advance.

"Kill the devils! Take the ship!"

We surged forward with such power I believed the impact of our bodies alone could flatten the barricade. Mere steps away from it, however, the ship abruptly bucked and rocked. The sails flapped and cracked as if every bit of rigging had snapped and the masts would be next.

Flung to the deck, we tumbled and tossed. Our roar splintered into howls of terror that rose in volume and pitch as the ship floundered ever more wildly, and we with it. Had Gwan Gung sent a storm at last?

Under a tangle of bodies and limbs, I struggled for breath. The load above me shifted, grinding my forehead and nose painfully against grit, hard wood. Heaving mightily, I arched my shoulders, my neck, my head, dislodging enough of the crush for a gust of life-giving air that brought the glorious words: "The ship is ours! We're homeward bound."

BA AND MA had insisted on leaving their sickbeds to welcome Fourth Brother-in-law home. The children, wakened from sleep by the bustle, had rushed to greet him. In the privy, I'd heard their joyful cries and dashed into the house believing I'd see my husband, too. At the shock of finding Fourth Brother-in-law without Ah Lung, I'd almost collapsed.

Listening to Fourth Brother-in-law tell all, I'd had to pinch my lips to keep from fainting. Then I had to lean against the altar and hold one trembling hand with the other before I could light incense to Heaven for guiding Moongirl to my husband.

I hoped the sandalwood smoke would restore me. Our worms, devouring ever larger quantities of mulberry, were expelling more and more waste, and it had become impossible for me to change the paper in their trays as often as I should. Now tendrils of musky odor were creeping into the wormhouse, polluting, and I needed to wash, change my clothes, and get back to work.

Even more, I needed my husband and, bowing my head, I again entreated Heaven to help him best the devils, to come home. Behind me, the family was plying Fourth Brother-in-law with questions.

"Weren't you afraid?"

"No, I was too full of thoughts about Ah Lung to have room for *any* feelings."

Twisting around to face Fourth Brother-in-law, I urged, "Apply that same principle in the wormhouse."

"Bo See," Fourth Sister-in-law snapped. "*My* husband is talking about *yours*! How can you bring up worms?"

"So Ah Lung won't come home to starve," Ba wheezed in a spasm of coughing.

Third Brother-in-law sprang from his stool and pounded Ba's back. Thrusting a spittoon at the nearest child to hold at the ready for Ba, Eldest Brother-in-law directed those wedged between his wife and the kitchen to open a path for her. Ma, too weak to help, even to speak, flailed her hands. On either side of her, Third and Fourth Sisters-in-law murmured soothingly.

Second Sister-in-law shuttered the window against drafts and late-night damp, then slipped through a crack in the quilt partition. At another click-click of shutter latches, I noticed the altar candles' flickering light intensify, a heightening in the aroma from the incense. Squinting and sniffing, I tried to gauge how much of the smoke was drifting into the rafters, whether the smell of sandalwood was strong enough to cling to the mulberry baskets on the other side, spoiling the next batch of leaves picked.

Abruptly, Ba hacked out a great gob of phlegm. Moments later, Eldest Sister-in-law hurried in with a bowl of fragrant orange-rind brew she'd heated. When she handed Ba the steaming bowl, he clasped it with both hands, closed his eyes, inhaled deeply.

How could I suggest moving the baskets into the courtyard without causing another upset, I wondered.

"Bo See," Ba rasped. "Explain yourself."

I repeated what I'd said over and over in the years since I'd come to Strongworm: "Inside the wormhouse, I think of nothing except our silkworms."

For the first time, Ba nodded understanding. "That's why you have no room for any feelings and can be calm."

"Before Ah Lung was kidnapped, I'd have laughed if anyone had told me I could be filled with thoughts of him alone," Fourth Brother-in-law admitted. "But worms?"

WHILE CARRYING BROKEN, blood-soaked mutineers to the devil-ship's sickroom, I'd noticed ruffians ransacking the cabins behind the barricade. Ah Jun, whose opera troupe had been kidnapped by pirates, later claimed he'd recognized one of their captors among these looters: a brute with a distinctive double-slash scar across a bulbous nose.

Other actors in the opera troupe not only confirmed this fellow's presence but that of several more pirates.

"I won't forget those lumps of filth if I live to be one hundred."

"Hum gah chaan, may their families be wiped out!"

"Killing is too good for them. Lahn tahn, may they be paralyzed and forced to crawl."

"Did you see the bastards filling the longboat with their plunder?"

"Yeah. Then that brute with the double-slash scar sounded the alarm, 'Man overboard' and bellowed, 'Lower the longboat!'"

"Tricky bastard!"

"I sure didn't hear any cry for help."

"Not even a splash."

"Not until that longboat hit water."

"That's strange," Ah Jook mused. "The villains usually wait until dark to make their getaway."

"What do you mean 'usually?'" Ah Jun demanded.

"In the boatyard where I worked, it was common knowledge that pirates sell themselves as piglets in order to rob devil-ships, and they always go about it the same way. They start a mutiny when they're within a few days sail of their lairs. . . ."

"Captives don't need pirates to get a mutiny going," Shorty jumped in.

Ah Jun agreed. "When we were imprisoned on the pirates' junk, we rose against them. We just weren't lucky enough to take over the vessel like we did here."

⁓

HUNDREDS OF MEN crowded the deck between the sick-room and the water cistern adjacent to the cookhouse.

"Bei hoi, get out of the way," I pleaded.

All that gave way was my voice, thin and cracked, but I was too thirsty to be polite, and I plunged into the noisy throng. Jovial as on a festival day, most of those I bumped ignored me, the few who raised a hand or voice in anger were easily soothed. I resisted the bangs and shoves that pushed me from my goal, welcomed whatever propelled me closer.

Slamming against the cistern, my pants provided little protection from the metal's heat. But I did not shrink back a jot. The water sloshed as invitingly as the pure, cool water I drew from our village well and, imitating those around me, I cupped my hands together despite their filth and dipped them in.

Beneath its glittering surface, the lukewarm water was streaked with blood as well as dirt and tasted foul. I drank scoop after scoop anyway. Then, my own thirst satisfied, I dove into the cookhouse, dug out a teapot, sidled, elbowed, and shouldered my way back to the water cistern, filled the pot for Scholar Mok.

The between-decks, although nearly empty, remained gloomy, the air fetid. With no one in my way, however, climbing onto the platform was easy. Kneeling beside Scholar Mok, I took my first close look at the man.

To my dismay, some son of a turtle had stolen his robe, socks, and shoes—everything except his pants. Moreover, the muddy gray of Scholar Mok's skin was frightening, and his odor rivaled that of the wastebuckets. Could he have soiled himself despite his fast? Or was I smelling decay because he was dead?

"Scholar Mok," I shouted above the footfalls overhead. "Scholar Mok!"

Accustomed now to the gloom, I saw his chest rise and fall, albeit very slightly, very slowly. Relieved, I persisted.

"Scholar Mok, you can drink. We're homeward bound."

I thrilled at the words "homeward bound," and it seemed to me Scholar Mok's eyelids fluttered. But his eyes had sunk so deep in their sockets that I might have been mistaken: When I dribbled water through his swollen lips, it spilled from the corners of his mouth, down the sides of his stubbled jaw.

Repeating, "Drink, we're homeward bound," I tried again.

This time, not a drop leaked. Encouraged, I carefully tipped in another dollop and another—only to realize when water started trickling out that it must be pooling in Scholar Mok's mouth.

"Swallow," I urged.

I checked his throat with my fingertips. In the stuffy heat, he was as drenched as myself. Where my skin was hot to the touch though, his felt chill, and I could detect no movement. Had Scholar Mok become too weak to swallow? If removed from this poisoned air, could he yet be restored?

Rocking back onto my heels, I considered who I could ask to help me carry him on deck. Not the sick groaning in their berths. Nor the gamblers trading insults, rowdy oaths. Should I. . . .

Celebratory firecrackers popped and crackled over-head, and at their merry din, my joy that I'd soon be home swelled, as did my pity for the men lost to their families forever.

~

QUESTIONED SEPARATELY, TWITCHY, the interpreter, and Ah Duk, the ship's carpenter, both insisted the captain had feared a mutiny from his sailors almost as much as from us. So the devil had not only forbidden them to gath-er and converse while on deck, but he'd broken the tips off their knives and hidden any weapons not in use. Then, the mutiny having taken the captain by surprise, he'd had no opportunity to distribute additional swords, muskets, or gunpowder before we overran the ship.

Except for Twitchy and Ah Duk, captain and crew were either chained and under guard or pinned aloft with the muskets in our possession. Should Twitchy and Ah Duk have been shackled, too? Maybe. As more than one man pointed out, the devil-English had won both wars over opium because Chinese evildoers had helped them by working as their translators, craftsmen, and guides.

But did that mean, as these same men contended, that Twitchy and Ah Duk had betrayed us? I don't know. The racket and confusion on deck was such that men standing side by side later argued over what they witnessed, and I was below.

This, though, is certain: The devils somehow managed to arm themselves, and the pops and crackles I heard weren't firecrackers but shots that set off a stampede.

"Ai yah!"

"Help! Gow meng ah!"

"Run!"

"Stand and fight!"

Murderous volleys from the cannons thundered over the cries of men leaping, diving, and flying through the three hatches. Too shocked to do anything else, I flung my arms over Scholar Mok's head, shielding it from the hands, feet, and knees of those madly scrambling into berths from the walkway.

The ship creaked and rocked under the cannons' roar. The platform beneath us shuddered ominously. Swathes of smelly, blinding dust swirled, strangling. Metal rasped and clanged against metal, and an iron band of dread clamped around my chest. Were the devils locking us in? Should I abandon Scholar Mok and answer the call to fight? Ai, was that the sound of splintering wood?

As the ship pitched, I clutched the board that edged the berth with one hand and held Scholar Mok down with the other, saving him from hurtling onto the walkway. But I could not protect him from the men tossed on top of us, crushing us.

"Diu!"

"Are you mad?"

Thump! Ding! Thump! Thump!

The next roll of the ship sent the men above us tumbling, and through the gloom, I made out shadows swarming the clogged walkway and platforms—realized there was no longer any gunfire in the hubbub.

Thump! Thump! Clink!

Were these sounds a signal like Corporal Woo's drumming?

Thump! Thump! Thump!

Still holding Scholar Mok steady, I turned around.

Ping! Thump! Thump! Thump!

In the narrow beams of straw-mottled sunlight streaming through the barred midship hatch, men were hurling up what looked like knives and bolts. A few of these objects catapulted out successfully, but most either fell short or hit metal, dropped back down—and were relaunched. Did any strike a devil?

Thump! Thump! Thump!

A knot of men farther along the walkway appeared to be clobbering the ceiling with a heavy pole.

Thump! Thump! Thump!

Light rimmed the planks under assault, and despite the resounding crash of the aft hatch slamming shut, I felt a sliver of hope that we might yet prevail. Determined to help make good that hope, I wedged Scholar Mok snugly among the men packing the platform.

Thump!

The battering ram smashed through the ceiling to cheers, a brilliant shaft of light, a rush of fresh salt air—torrents of water, bellows, squawks, and yowls. I jumped into the seething mass of men in the walkway.

"Watch out!"

The blow to the side of my head was glancing, and I did not sink into the fray but sprawled on top, flailing like an upturned turtle. Buffeted, clawed, and kicked by men who were similarly struggling to right themselves, I rolled as the ship lunged—saw the force of the water gushing down was preventing anybody from climbing out.

"Cut that pisser!"

Makeshift spears thrust through the hole fell short of the hose.

"Smash the pump!"

How? The ladder to the waterpump in the hold passed through the between-decks, but it was on the other side of thick iron bars.

"Let me through!"

"Make way for the boxing master."

Here was something I could do. Crawling into an already crammed lower berth, I folded into myself so more men could worm in, opening a path for the boxing master.

⌐⌐

I HOPED BUT did not believe the boxing master could wrench open the thick iron bars. Sure boxing masters possess superhuman strength and can move like swimming dragons, stare like watchful monkeys, sit like crouching tigers, turn like hovering eagles. In our market town I'd even seen boxing masters, armed with nothing except these techniques, soundly defeat opponents brandishing swords and spears. If this boxing master possessed these skills and strength, however, wouldn't he have broken free of his captors long ago? At the very least, his expertise would've made him stand out during the takeover of the ship.

True, I'd only caught snatches of the fighting, and now the platform I'd squashed onto was sagging, the one above, too, knocking me into. . . .

Sticky dampness.

The loathsome taste of sludge.

Silence pricked with loud hurt.

Huzzas.

Unspeakable pain.

Mewls.

Mine?

⁓

SQUEAKS.　　　.

Nails grazing skin.

Scritch-scratch, scritch-scratch, scritch. . . .

"Torch the ship!"

"You crazy?"

"Yut wok sook, we'll all be cooked!"

"You want to visit the Sea Dragon? Go!"

"I'll kill you first."

"Lam ju sei lah, then we'll die together."

Metal clashing, hissing into flesh.

Grunts.

Shrieks of rage and pain.

The thick, hot smell of blood.

WHIFFS OF SMOKE.

Dark forms tinged red.

Blood-stained warriors?

Firebrands?

Fiends from Hell?

Savages maybe.

Or men acting savage in order to do good.

"FIRE!"

"Fire!"

Panicked hollers.

Blistering heat.

Harsh fumes from burning pitch, singed hair and skin.

Splashes and splatters.

Dense, suffocating smoke.

Cries for mercy.

Wordless wails.

Moans.

Rivers of sweat carrying me home.

～～

PORK ONLY TOUCHED our family's lips at festivals, when every adult male in Strongworm received a portion of the meat his clan used in ritual sacrifices to the Ancestors.

Where village elders and wealthy members of a clan could expect up to eight catties of this meat, the men in poor families like ours were limited to one.

"The wealthy already have plenty," Moongirl had protested as a child.

"Plenty isn't enough for them," Ba had huffed. "They always want more. They make sure they get it, too, by forcing us deeper and deeper into their debt. . . ."

"Be thankful we don't owe Old Bloodsucker," Ma had cut in quietly but firmly. "Otherwise we'd have to surrender every scrap of our pork to him."

Ba was, of course, thankful. We all were. But our family's share of meat wasn't enough to fill the cracks between our teeth, and the months until we'd taste pork again seemed to stretch forever.

Sometimes my longing for pork would grow so great that I'd keep an ear cocked for the squeals and screams of pigs. I'd race to watch them rounded up and slaughtered, then post myself where I could see the gutted pigs lowered into our Ancestral Hall's large brick oven.

The firebox at the bottom of this oven was completely sealed off so no fire or smoke would touch the meat. Just above the firebox, there was a small opening for a pan to catch the drippings.

At the sizzle of fat on the metal, I'd savor the rich aroma from the roasting pigs. I'd imagine sinking my teeth into the pigs' delicious skin, the hot fat squirting out, coating my tongue, sliding thick and warm down my throat as the crackling crumbled, giving way to velvet flesh.

Not once did I think of the pigs: how the animals selected for slaughter used to resist entering their holding pens; how they had to be tricked and prodded and struck; how the pigs' struggles inevitably failed to save them from their fate.

~~⌐

IN THE BETWEEN-decks, my struggles ended when I was felled by the platform's collapse. But there were men who, taking their lead from fleeing rats, wriggled out the airpipes. Others continued tearing away supports from platforms, then ramming the posts against the planks overhead until they crashed through to the deck.

After the boxing master wrenched open the iron bars to the waterpump and smashed it, some men squirmed out these holes as well. Cutting off the water supply to the devils' hose did not really help our cause though. Men could only emerge onto the deck one by one, and the devils captured all as easily as if they were plucking onions out of a field.

In desperation, the boldest and rashest among us attempted to force our release by torching the ship. The devils, instead of throwing open the hatches, covered both the hatch grates *and* the holes in the deck. This turned the between-decks into a sweltering oven but did little to put out the fire, and had there not been men who doused the flames with piss then snuffed out the embers with wet jackets, the ship might well have burned to the water, and us with it. Indeed, I've since heard of captains and crews abandoning burning devil-ships and sailing to safety in longboats while men trapped in the between-decks either roasted or drowned.

I am grateful we were spared such horror. Before the devils uncovered the hatch grates, however, over one hundred of us had suffocated to death, and the survivors, to a man, were too weak to resist the devils' probes for weapons—such as pins, razors, and blades—small enough to be hidden in hair, cavities, folds of flesh.

⁓

AH MING MAINTAINED that just as the devils were deliberately weakening those who accepted their offers of opium by smothering the smokers' spirits, the captain had robbed the between-decks of air to extinguish the fire in us. Ah Ming also insisted our mutiny had been doomed from the start because the sails on foreign vessels cannot be manipulated from the deck like those on a junk.

Yes, mutineers had made the devil-sailors climb the masts at gunpoint, and I'd thought that sufficient to make true the glorious words, "The ship is ours." But our helmsman, although a Tanka capable of navigating the ship, could not give the orders necessary for working the complicated maze of rigging. None of our men could. So our helmsman had relied on the captain and Red, which meant control of the devil-ship had never actually left their hands.

The captain, having crushed our mutiny, had the debris removed from the between-decks but did not repair any of the platforms, leaving us squeezed skin-to-skin in spite of our reduced numbers. He personally selected the strongest looking among the survivors of his slaughter for the full forty-eight lashes stipulated for mutineers, and he ordered the men whipped while lying face down on sacks of rice, then shackled in pairs and sent below.

Under Red's supervision, sacks saturated with blood were quickly replaced; the devil-sailors carrying out the punishment were kept fresh through rotation. The prostrate men, beaten senseless, were revived with buckets of seawater, their raw backs salted and vinegared.

My own senses, lost in the platform's collapse, had not

then fully returned. But those who witnessed this punishment shuddered when speaking of it, and many screamed as loudly in their sleep as the men who'd been flogged.

The blood-soaked rice was boiled—without rinsing a single grain—for our meals. Anybody who refused to eat was force-fed through a bamboo tube, and the taste of blood, the men's groans, the never-ending clank of chains underscored our defeat.

Armed devils took over the corporals' duties. Through Twitchy, these devils ordered us to drop onto our haunches the moment we reached the deck. Moving forward on a sloping, rolling deck while squatting, we tumbled against them, each other, and to avoid the devils' snarls and harsh blows, we had to approach the cookhouse on our hands and knees.

Once burdened with tea and rice for ten, we were allowed to walk. But the falling platforms had broken several of my ribs, and although Ah Ming had bound my chest tight with his extra pair of pants, breathing still felt like sticking needles into my chest. When I carried our rations, the needles turned into knives. Rasping as though I were winded rather than in pain, I made no complaint. I was too desperate for the brief release from the between-decks that my job as steward afforded.

Not for a moment, not even in my sleep, however, could I escape Moongirl's lament which had, with the mutiny's failure, begun sweeping over me in melancholy waves:

"Savages have taken you prisoner.

Once you leave the country,

There will be no return.

You will strain your eyes

Looking for your dear ones,

But your dear ones will not appear.

You will strain your ears

Listening for your dear ones,

But you will not hear their steps.

Alone among strangers and barbarians,

Your sorrow will grow bigger than a mountain,

Your tears will fall like rain.

Only by clever planning

Can the situation be turned around."

WITH FOURTH BROTHER-IN-LAW working beside me in the wormhouse, there was, once again, only the clean odor of freshly cut leaves. There were no impatient worms clambering over each other in search of mulberry, leaving agonized writhing or stiff little corpses in their wake.

The worms did stop eating after a few days. Happily, it was because they were ready to start spinning, and from the short threads they'd been discharging when shifting to better grasp a piece of mulberry or cast off old skin, I knew the single long strands for their cocoons would be the best quality silk: glossy *and* strong.

As always, I alone examined our cocoons. Setting aside the whitest, smoothest, and thickest, I made sure I had the right proportion of the male, which were small and pointed at each end, and the female, which were round and soft. Then, while my brothers-in-law placed the remaining cocoons over a slow, steady heat, I began raising a new generation of worms. I also kept a close eye on the cocoons I'd chosen. And when the moths emerged, I removed the ones with crumpled wings, red bellies, or dry tails—any sign the creatures might produce less than perfect worms. I brought together the moths that emerged the same day to mate, then set the females onto squares of paper to lay their eggs.

I'd long ago counseled families in Strongworm to follow my strategy. "If you choose cocoons throughout a season rather than wait to get all from the final generation, you'll have more of a selection *and* you'll be certain you won't get caught short."

They'd protested that they were already stretched to the limit raising worms and had no time for culling cocoons or arranging the mating of moths until a season's end. Some women had even suggested I was overanxious about eggs because I was still without child:

"You're afraid you'll stay childless."

"With good reason since Ah Lung shared his mother's belly with a girl. That was bound to have weakened his male energy."

"Moongirl leaped out ahead of Ah Lung, you know."

"Giving Moongirl the formal name Yuet Fung, Moon Phoenix, was alright but what was their father thinking when he chose Yuet Lung, Moon Dragon, for a son? The moon's female influences were bound to further dilute the dragon's manly energies!"

Ah Lung and I, confident of children in our future, had made a game out of this talk. Flushing hot, I'd brazenly ask him to pleasure me. He'd stammer that he couldn't because he'd been unmanned. Ever so tenderly I'd stroke his dragon in pretended sorrow, and, ai, how he'd have to struggle to keep it from waking! How we'd laugh and play when he failed.

Two bowls of tea a day could not slake anyone's thirst, and on those occasions the sky ripped open while I was fetching our rations or swilling teapot and bowls, I did not run for shelter as I would have in Strongworm. Like the other stewards, I threw back my head and opened my mouth so the rain could drench my aching throat as if it were a parched field. I'd savor the rain's sweetness—even as growls, vicious pokes and prods from our guards were driving us below.

Some of these same devils were smuggling water into the between-decks for sale to those who somehow still had cash. Not surprisingly, thieves became as commonplace as the bugs sucking our blood. Bickering exploded into fierce quarrels, brutal fights.

Yes, thieves and fighters risked the lash. But devil-guards accepted bribes as readily as piggy-corporals, and those punished could count on their floggings to stop after twelve strokes, their lacerated backs to eventually heal. Thirst was a torture without end.

During storms, the crew dropped down buckets of hard biscuits without a drop of water and fit raincloths over the hatches, sealing us into suffocating darkness. Rain pelting the deck and the sea lashing over the ship's sides gushed through seams in the planks, soaking us to the bone. Despite the steady wheeze and clank of the ship's pump, bilge welled up from below.

There was water enough that men thrown into the walkways sometimes drowned, and many argued that the puddles in our berths, although brackish, were safe for drinking. But few managed more than a few licks: The ship was sheering in mountainous seas, threatening to capsize, and we were clinging to the platforms and each other, howling like the wind shrieking through the rigging.

Then, too, we all had raw patches from the constant grinding of skin against wood, and it wasn't unusual for the punching and pounding to tear off long strips of soggy skin and mangle limbs beyond repair. Many a belly, heaving with the swells, actively rebelled, adding to our torments.

After the seas calmed and the crew peeled back the raincloths, waterlogged timbers steamed foul vapors for days. Since sunlight only reached wood directly under the hatches, most berths remained moist. So did men who never went above as stewards or for opium.

This damp gave rise to burning fevers, hacking coughs. Everybody suffered from loose bowels. With maggots infesting our blood-streaked rice, meat that was either souring or already putrid, some men started passing blood.

The doctor reserved the four beds in the sickroom for those with diseases that might spread to others. Compelled to stay in the airless swamp of the between-decks, few men recovered. Those who became too enfeebled to leave their berths or use a spittoon soiled themselves, the platforms, their neighbors.

While above, I frequently heard scraping and hammering. I spotted sailors mucking out the animals' pens, toiling with brushes, stitching torn canvas, sewing new sails, taking apart ropes, or replacing worn rigging. I breathed air redolent with varnish, paint, hot tar. Yet the captain repeatedly refused our petitions for buckets, water, and brushes with which to clean below.

Washing up from meals, I'd slip into the water the scraps of cloth that Ah Ming had ripped from his pants after my ribs mended. On my return, I'd wipe the faces and the wood beneath the nearest invalids until the cloths, stiff with all manner of waste, did more harm than good.

Throughout the between-decks, other stewards were doing likewise. Nevertheless, filth crusted flesh and wood. Boils erupted. Sores festered, some oozed pus. Frightful odors of decay poisoned every breath.

Then cholera swooped down on us, and the doctor ordered buckets of purifying lime sloshed over the platforms, the slippery sludge of rotting straw, shit, and piss in the walkways. Ai, that lime bit into our skin, our nostrils! But it did little to loosen cholera's grip: Even doubling men up, the doctor ran out of beds in the sickroom.

When attacked, men complained of burning heat although their skin felt clammy cold. Plagued by agonizing cramps that preceded violent bouts of vomiting and spurting bowels, their color turned from lead to a liverish red, then a dark, deep blue.

None of those felled survived. Death, though, came swiftly. In truth, were it not for my family, I would have welcomed it.

Fourth Brother-in-law confessed it wasn't thoughts of worms but our being shorthanded that enabled him to remain calm in our wormhouse. "Going from one task to another has me completely absorbed!"

Pouncing on this insight, I brought enough workers back to the wormhouse to provide our worms with the best of care but not so many that anyone ever had an idle moment for disturbing thoughts or feelings to surface.

"Good," Eldest Sister-in-law praised. "Now you can stop making do with the odd mouthful of rice and return to eating properly with us twice a day."

Eldest Brother-in-law encouraged me to take longer, more frequent breaks, too. Outside our wormhouse, however, my mind hopped like a restless monkey, my heart pounded like a galloping horse: Were the captives on the devil-ship in rebellion? Had Ah Lung been injured or escaped unscathed? Had he reached Moongirl in Canton? Was he on his way home?

EVEN IF MY wife's calm in the wormhouse prevailed, as I hoped and prayed it would, Bo See had no control over outside forces, and during the long silk season, heavy rains brought by big winds could last for days, days in which our worms would go hungry if the family failed to pick sufficient leaves or the fussy creatures refused to eat the stored mulberry because they preferred fresh. Often dikes collapsed, flooding fields. Then the standing water could rot the very roots of the mulberry on which our worms depended. And landlords calculated rents on the percentage of an anticipated harvest. They collected every copper owed regardless of the actual result. In truth, they were constantly pressing their feet against our necks, sometimes lightly, sometimes grinding our faces into the mud. If I could survive the horrors of this devil-ship, though, Ba would have my earnings to pay off our debts *and* buy fields, throwing the landlords from our necks forever.

Already I could hear Ba, on receiving my first remittance, shout, "Come! Come quick!" to Ma, my brothers and their wives, my own wife, our nephews and nieces. "Ah Lung's alive!"

Then, while Bo See and Ma lit incense to Heaven for keeping me safe, the rest of the family would gaze at the silver in wide-eyed wonder, exclaiming:

"Wah!"

"Ah Lung really took Moongirl's lament to heart."

"What do you mean?"

"Don't you remember? Moongirl added the lines 'Only by clever planning can the situation be turned around.'"

"She meant for Ah Lung to find a way home."

"And he says in his letter that he *will*—but only after he's made enough to turn *our* situation around."

⁓

AGAIN AND AGAIN my eyes scoured the river, and at the shape of my husband's head, the curve of his shoulders silhouetted on the deck of a sampan, my heart would fly out to meet him—only to stop dead when Ah Lung himself did not appear.

Fighting a burgeoning panic, I reasoned: Even free of his devil-captors, Ah Lung would be beggared, friendless, lost among foreigners. How could he make his way home as swiftly as we expected? He might not be back until our eggs hatched for the seventh and final generation of the season.

Or the worms entered their first sleep.

Their second.

Their third.

Their fourth.

Or they formed cocoons.

Or the moths burrowed out and mated.

⁓

I'D BEEN CAPTURED while our family was raising our fifth generation of worms. By my reckoning, the silk season had ended. Ba would be talking to my brothers about draining our fish ponds, harvesting the fish, and dredging up the mud at the bottom.

This mud—rich from the nightsoil and worm waste that we fed the fish as well as their own droppings—was perfect for fertilizing our fields. Digging up the muck was smelly, filthy, backbreaking work, however, and my brothers hated the chore. Until my marriage, I had too.

In the years since, I'd looked forward to it. Bo See and I had no chance to see each other unclothed in the full light of day. Before shoveling mud from our ponds, though, I'd shed my jacket, roll my pants up to my thighs, and Bo See, bringing water out to me, would caress my legs with her gaze. Despite the rank smells steaming from the muck, she'd linger to watch my muscles swell, ripple up my arms, and across my back. If no one else was near, she'd even unbutton the stiff collar that hugged her neck, revealing the delicate hollow where throat meets chest, and hike her long, loose pants above her shapely ankles and calves, exposing pale, smooth skin.

Lest we draw the attention of someone passing, we never spoke. Nor did we dare touch. But our eyes, meeting, would burn with remembered pleasure, impatience for the joyful play night would bring.

⌒

EVERY AUTUMN, AH Lung would pick bak yuk lan blossoms for me on his way home from the family's ponds. I'd tuck them into my bun, and their heady scent would tease deliciously as we ate our evening meal, perfume our bed when at last we unpinned my hair for play.

In anticipation of my husband's return, I laid fresh bak yuk lan on his pillow. Each time their fragrance faded and the soft white petals curled brittle brown, I plucked more.

AT HOME, MEN in mourning did not shave the crowns of their heads, and it seemed fitting to me that on the devil-ship, we had the shaggy, unkempt look of mourners: The captain had sailed from Macao with almost eight-hundred captives; in sight of Peru, the count did not reach five hundred.

Moreover, we'd been stolen for our strength. But when the devils drove us on deck after four months at sea, many were too debilitated to climb the ladders, or they collapsed on deck from the effort. Others, when hosed with salt water, toppled under the force of the stream.

I could still pick up the fallen and carry them beyond reach of the hose. While scraping the grime from my limbs, though, I easily circled my thighs with both hands, my upper arms with one, and my chest felt as deeply ridged as a new washboard. Would I have to waste precious months in a fatteninghouse?

Twitchy, quivering and blinking as much as ever, had explained that ships cannot enter Callao's harbor until a health officer, having inspected the vessel and all on board, declared them clean. So our quarters would be scrubbed while we washed. The platforms destroyed in the mutiny would be repaired. Our clothes, rotted into rags, would be replaced with new jackets and pants.

"Once the ship has sailed into the harbor, you'll line up on deck by your berth numbers. Buyers will take the numbered tags from the necks of those whose contracts they wish to purchase, and after they've finished making their selections, you'll board boats that will ferry you to shore.

"Don't be alarmed if you're too thin or infirm to attract a buyer. There are fatteninghouses in Callao where you can regain your health with rest and good food."

"Ahhh," purred Big Belly.

A fevered bag of sagging skin and bones, Big Belly couldn't stand without support. But he'd outlived Toothless, Ah Jook, and Sleepy.

Ah Ming, too, was gone, and when I hoisted Big Belly onto my back and up the ladder, he gurgled into my ear, "Didn't . . . I . . . say . . . I'm . . . lucky?"

In the past ten days, I'd noticed more and more birds when going above as steward: little three-inch sooty puffs that walked on water; dusky brown goose-necked creatures with wingspans of nine or ten feet; birds the size of pigeons; some that looked like crows; others that flew low like ducks. So I wasn't startled by the thousands of birds darkening an otherwise dazzling sky, cawing and shrilling plaints. Big Belly scrabbled weakly at my neck, my back.

"The birds won't harm you," I soothed as I lowered him into a sheltered area near the sickroom. "The devils won't bother you either. They have their hands full working the pump and hose and guarding the sides of the ship."

Still Big Belly fumbled at my ankles. Had my assurances been drowned in bird cries, the thunderous racket of men released at last from close confinement?

"I'll come back to wash you soon as I scrub off the worst of my dirt," I promised in a shout. "Otherwise I'll just be adding mine to yours."

MINDFUL OF MY promise to Big Belly, I washed my hair without taking time to unravel all the snarls, rinsed it in vinegar-water to kill any remaining lice, then headed back to the sickroom.

My hair clung wetly to my neck, shoulders, and back. Water, black with filth, swirled around my ankles. Jostling through the crush on the main deck, I could only take small steps. Even so, I splattered men newly clean who grumbled and cursed despite my repeated apologies.

After the main mast, there was less water, fewer men,

and I quickened my pace. To my bewilderment, Big Belly wasn't where I'd left him. Had he crawled inside the sick-room to flee the birds or the encroaching water?

I scanned floor and beds from the doorway. The room was completely empty. Could someone be washing the sick on the other side of the ship? Had they included Big Belly?

Darting over to a little round window, I poked my head out: Two brawny sailors were tying heavy stones around Big Belly's ankles as if he were a corpse.

"No!" I cried. "He's alive."

But Big Belly was already in the air, plummeting into the sea. At the splash, birds that had been bobbing in the water screeched and wheeled up in a wild scramble of beating wings. Red, roaring at the sailors, pointed towards another wraith leaking piteous tears.

If there were others from the between-decks who witnessed these killings, they said nothing as the devil-ship sailed into Callao. I, too, was silent. Speaking among ourselves saved no one, and speaking to murdering devils could only bring more trouble.

But I wondered: Could the captain's desperate attempts to hide his deviltry from Peruvian officials mean *they* were a civilized people?

Certainly the Peruvians' provision of fatteninghouses showed generosity. And the between-decks, readied for their inspection, smelled of soap, pitch, and freshly strewn straw; instead of cupping together like spoons, we could at last lie flat on our backs.

Moreover, we'd always been issued hard biscuits and water, then locked below as the ship headed into port. In Callao, we'd be going above even before our contracts were purchased.

Surely these changes signified that Peruvians would, at the very least, treat us fairly. After I earned enough silver to make my family comfortable, perhaps my master would let me buy out the balance of my contract and go home early!

First, I had to attract a buyer.

～

MY VIEW OF shore was obscured by dozens of two- and three-masted vessels surrounding the ship, the rise and fall of the deck beneath my feet, the orderly rows of men ahead of me, on either side. But I did not care. Lively as a silkworm changing its skin, I was shedding my jacket, as Twitchy had instructed, studying the pale-faced, white-clad buyers swarming through our ranks, twirling men like tops, tapping chests, squeezing limbs.

With the intensity of a gambler shrewdly calculating his odds, I noted who the buyers chose, who they refused, and as one approached me, I arranged my face in the docile expression that gentry back home also preferred. To demonstrate my strength, I did not ball my hands into fists or stamp my feet; I flexed the muscles in my arms while running in place. The instant he reached out to turn me, I spun around to show I was quick-witted and just as my wrists bore no marks from shackles, my back wasn't scarred by whips. Docile as a girl offering proof of sound teeth and sweet breath to a matchmaker, I opened my mouth for examination. Although his fingers pressed hard on my sore gums, I neither yelped nor winced.

Yanking my numbered tag, the buyer signified his approval, and as the twine bit into my neck before snapping, I offered a prayer of thanks to the God of Luck.

Seated across from Moongirl at the table, Ba extended both arms, emphasizing he wasn't just speaking for himself but for his sons to his left, his wife and me to his right.

"We've come to accept Ah Lung must have failed to escape from the devil-ship."

Secretly, I still cherished the hope Ah Lung was making his way home, and despite Ba's declaration, he and the others must have as well, for at Moongirl's sharp nod of agreement, every face around the table reflected my own dismay. Ba's arms dropped heavily, his teeth ground. Ma's eyes leaked tears.

Moongirl urged us not to despair. "Canton traders say that free Chinese in Peru intercede on behalf of countrymen laboring under contracts—just like the God of Luck did for enslaved dwarves when he was a mortal."

Ma brightened. "May these free Chinese soon secure the release—"

"No," Moongirl interrupted. "The contracts are binding and can't be broken. But free Chinese speak out against mistreatment. So Ah Lung won't be friendless, and once we receive a letter from him, we can send advice for how he can best preserve his strength until his contract expires and he *is* released."

Her parents and brothers seized this bone. I could not. Murmuring, "I'll get more tea," I bolted into the kitchen.

Eldest Sister-in-law, coming in from the courtyard with more kindling, gave me a questioning look. I picked up the teapot, returned to the main room and circled the table, pouring tea.

From the kitchen, kindling in the stove snapped and popped as loud as the talk around me. Suddenly, there was a hiss of fat, prolonged sizzling.

Moongirl reared up like a silkworm sensing the approach of tender, sweet mulberry. "Aaaah, fried chrysalids."

For the first time since Ah Lung's capture, Third Brother-in-law's eyes sparkled with mischief, and he mock wailed in his sister's higher pitch, "Hurry, Eldest Sister-in-law! My mouth is watering."

The corners of Second Brother-in-law's lips twitched from suppressed laughter. "Third Brother, where did the chrysalids come from?"

"When our wives stopped reeling yesterday, they drained their cauldrons of water, scooped out the chrysalids at the bottom, and spread them to dry so Eldest Sister-in-law could cook them today."

"Then shouldn't *they* be the ones to enjoy the treat, not Moongirl?"

As Moongirl, her parents, and brothers burst into laughter, Eldest Sister-in-law entered with a heaping platter of glistening chrysalids fried to a crisp, Second Brother-in-law grabbed a pair of chopsticks from the center of the table, lifted it to his lips, and tooted long trumpet blasts.

I retreated to the bed I'd shared with my husband. "Have you begun the labor for which you were stolen?" I asked him. "Is your master kind?"

DURING THE TEN days' sail from Callao to the dunghill where I labor, gray islands rose out of the sea, spouted water, then vanished; silver-winged fish leaped into the air and flew like birds; enormous brown-pelted, bewhiskered slugs barked like dogs and swam like fish.

The talk of men squeezed alongside me on the sloop's deck was no less bewildering. Plumped in fatteninghouses, they said these places are *not* run by generous benefactors for charity but greedy speculators who purchase the buyers' leavings on the cheap in hopes of selling them later at a profit. Furthermore, if health officers find contagion on a ship coming into port, the vessel is placed under quarantine for up to thirty days, thirty days in which all on board must be fed and watered at the captain's expense. But there are companies that guarantee cargoes, and since these companies pay the owners of devil-ships in full for their dead, it profits the captains to cram as many captives as they can into their between-decks, spend as little as possible on the men's care, then throw the near-dead into the sea before arrival.

Listening to these revelations, I became so agitated I chewed the insides of my cheeks until I tasted blood. Men obviously in the same state of bewildered distress asked whether there are companies that pay compensation for dead laborers in Peru.

The answer, although no, offered little relief since it included this: A master's profits so exceeds the cost of his laborers that most are as careless with lives as the captains of the devil-ships.

On the sloop, I clung to the word "most," the possibility of a kind master, silver I could send home. Upon landing, however, it became clear that in winning the approval of my buyer, I was no different from a silkworm spinning its own coffin, and much as I want to believe I can yet break out of the darkness and fly free, I fear I'll die in the service of my master.

⁓

RESPONSIBILITY FOR THE wormhouse excuses me from reeling cocoons, even those from a season's final generation of worms. As a girl, though, I'd learned to simultaneously throw multiple cocoons into a basin of boiling water to dissolve the stickiness binding the silk, pluck out the separated strands, spool them into a single strong thread, and when I offer to help my sisters-in-law reel, they accept.

Compelled to stand inches from the crackling fire, my thighs soon burn. Bending into the suffocating clouds of steam rising above the basin, my face drips sweat, melts. My fingers, dipping in and out of the scalding water, turn pink and tender as boiled shrimp. The concentration necessary to keep the strands from tangling or breaking wraps my head in a vise.

I welcome these discomforts. They help deaden the pain of my husband's absence.

⁓

THE ENORMOUS BARKING slugs are, I've learned, sea lions. Their droppings and those of birds are called *guano* in Spanish. And so effective is this guano supposed to be as fertilizer that, although there are five-hundred diggers on this island, we can't get ahead of the demand; there are always well over a hundred ships from around the world waiting—most for two or even three months—to be loaded.

At night we have a respite from the head-splitting clamor of the sea lions and birds. But even in sleep, the sharp, pisslike smell of guano pinches my nose, eyes, and throat, and when I begin digging at dawn, a dank, dense mist wraps around my bones. By midmorning, the sun burns off the last trace of mist, the heat grows stifling as the days before a big wind, my chest threatens to burst from lack of air.

The clouds overhead, resembling sheets of pale smoke, are too thin and hang too high in the sky to provide any ease from the sun's arrows, any hint of rain, and I long for them to turn dark and heavy, then shatter in brilliant flashes of lightning and thunderclaps, letting loose a deluge. But no rain falls here. That's why droppings beyond reach of the pounding surf don't wash away, why these gray, treeless hills and steep cliffs are solid guano, the sharp, pisslike smell so pervasive.

There are actually three islands. On the largest, North Island, diggers have labored for twenty years, and the hills are scarred by deep cuts. Still they rise a hundred feet and more above the sea, every bit as high as the hills here on Middle Island, which is half as large and has been worked half as long. As for South Island, its rounded hills— untouched by diggers and swarming with thousands of noisy sea lions and birds—are continuing to grow.

Flocks of birds, some as large as these dunghills, darken the sky. When overhead, the relief their shadows cast is as merciful as if Gwoon Yum herself has come.

"Look," I cry. "Take pity on us! Tell a bird—say one of those with a pouch hanging from a beak the length of my arm—to swoop down—"

Before I can complete my plea, the flock passes, shrilling and cawing, the sun hits with renewed venom, and I rebuke myself yet again for my foolishness, my inability to accept that here we are beyond Gwoon Yum's reach, beyond that of Fook Sing Gung, every God in Heaven.

Tightening my grip on the sweat-slick handle of the pickaxe, I swing. As the axe arcs, lightning streaks up my arms and across my shoulders; my heart thrashes against my ribs. Then the axe strikes ground, and my whole body judders. Grit nettles my calves. Chalky powder spirals up, thickening the haze from hundreds of axes hammering the hard-packed guano, shovels tossing crumbling clods through screens, filling baskets and wheelbarrows with the dust, dust that clogs my nostrils, seeps through my lips, coats my tongue, settles in my throat.

My eyes, afire, flood. Snorting and coughing, I swipe at them with the sodden rag around my neck. Nothing clears. I cannot see beyond my hands and feet. But the devils driving us have eyes like hawks, the strength to send us spinning with a kick, to cut us down with their rawhide whips, and although my arms protest, I raise my axe, bring it down.

PEDRO CHUFAT, WHO runs the store on North Island, wears a western-style straw hat and hard leather shoes, Chinese jacket and pants. He has the gold teeth, long nails, and excess flesh of a prosperous, middle-aged merchant, the leathery hands of a man once familiar with labor.

Every seventh day, Chufat brings over merchandise and sets up a stall for a few hours in the late afternoon. His goods are overpriced, poor in quality, and often damaged. With no one else to buy from, however, we diggers push ourselves hard to finish our day's work so we can go, and no matter how much Chufat brings, he always sells out.

Each time a shipment of pigs arrives to replace dead diggers, Chufat trots out an oily apology and string of excuses for his new customers while making brisk sales to old. His stream of patter is even swifter than his trade, and those making translations into other dialects sometimes slur, tripping over words in their efforts to keep pace.

"I'm ashamed of the mold and waterstains and rust. Really I am. But you know how leaky the foreigners' ocean-going vessels are, how everything in the coastal sloops that carried you here from Callao gets drenched in spray, and reducing prices is out of the question. I've got so many expenses beyond the cost of the goods, which is plenty high after shipping.

"There's the rent I have to pay to the *comandante* in charge of North Island. Then the boatmen who row me across the strait want their share. And the devil who rules this dunghill demands as much for this stall space as I give the *comandante* for a store!

"Between them all, I barely scrape by. I ask you, what fool except myself, a former pig who's experienced your misery, would have abandoned a thriving business on the mainland to bring you and your brothers on North Island these small comforts?"

"Don't you mean what fool would buy from you except a captive?" a wiry new arrival asks tartly.

Many grumble agreement.

Chufat, oozing understanding, says, "I was an angry pig, too. Stick around and I'll tell you how this piggy got away."

Diggers who've heard his story leave as soon as they've made their purchases. Most—clutching their packets of incense, dried fruit, twists of tobacco, bottles of balm, or tins of opium—shamble off silently. Some grouse that

Chufat likes the sound of his own voice as much as he does his profits, that he's a blowhard, a cheat.

I'm no less skeptical of Chufat, and my back and legs ache for bed. Nevertheless, I always stay. Later, I break Chufat's story into sections that I examine as closely as if I were Bo See studying our silkworms tray by tray, looking for anything that might be amiss or improved.

⁓

CHUFAT WAS ONE of seventy-five pigs purchased by a broker for a sugarcane plantation in a fertile river valley between this rainless coast's dark, forbidding cliffs and the distant cloud-topped mountains.

The pigs, on their arrival at the plantation, assembled in front of a hook-nosed white man who informed them—through an aloof, smooth-tongued interpreter—that he, their *patron*, had bought their labor for eight years and they'd be locked in at night to make sure they didn't steal what was now his.

"You'll be paid in scrip which you can spend in the plantation store. This store is well stocked with everything you Chinese enjoy, even opium. But I give you fair warning. The days you fail to complete your assigned tasks will be counted as sick days. All sick days will be added to your length of service.

"If you have any ideas about running, I advise you to

forget them. The overseers take roll call each morning, and I keep a detailed description of each worker. Should you be foolish enough to attempt escape despite my counsel, I will post your description in handbills and newspaper advertisements along with the offer of a generous reward for your return.

"There are skilled man-catchers who earn their livings from tracking down runaway Chinese. These man-catchers will chase you down, and when they bring you in, which I assure you they will, you'll be severely punished. Naturally, your length of service will also have to be extended to cover my expenses in getting you back and the days you're missing."

Even as the *patron* was talking, a devil big as an ox and black as soy sauce hauled in a scrawny runaway by his queue. The runaway, bruised purple from head to toe, was whipped by a black-skinned devil-driver until his back resembled pulverized meat. Then, for the next thirty days, the runaway was forced to cut cane while heavily chained.

⁓

THE MAN WHO purchased my contract in Callao was likewise a broker. We diggers are also paid in scrip. The devils that drive us are black, too.

Chufat says that for hundreds of years, black-skinned men, women, and children were stolen from Africa and carried across the seas chained in devil-ships, but the

Africans who were enslaved in Peru have all been freed. Certainly our drivers act like bitter wives who, on becoming mothers-in-law, avenge their past abuse on their daughters-in-law. Every one of the devils is quick to slice open a digger's flesh with their whips, and they leap to carry out the cruelest orders of our devil-king.

This creature—white and treacherous as the shit-covered rocks encircling the three Islands—rules all, and he has a standing order for the drivers to shackle any digger who breaks a tool, even by accident.

Of course, a digger in shackles has to hold up his chains with one hand while walking, otherwise the metal will gall his ankles. Like the rest of us, though, he has to carry his basket or push his wheelbarrow, heaped high with guano, to the depot for loading onto ships.

The distance, depending on where we're digging, can be as great as a quarter mile. Still the digger in chains must deliver the usual five tons—that's at least one-hundred loads, two-hundred treks back and forth—before he can stop for the day. If he fails, a devil will drive him with repeated lashings to the devil-king.

The digger will then be offered a choice: He can be chained overnight onto a pinnacle of rock where he'll be battered by the surf and risk tumbling into the sea; or he can be shackled to a skiff with a hole in the bottom, so he has to bail nonstop or drown.

In truth, these are not punishments but tortures which

pleasure the devil-king, and more than one digger has been pushed beyond endurance into madness.

⌒

CHUFAT LIKES TO boast, "The conditions I endured on the plantation were equally harsh. And under my *patron's* system of accounting, no pig was ever released from labor unless he became too old or weak or crippled to be useful. Still, I recognized I was lucky."

Those hearing him for the first time gasp. The tone of those providing translations into other dialects betrays their shock. I vow yet again to make Chufat's luck mine.

On every side diggers demand:

"Explain yourself."

"How were you lucky?"

"Because I didn't have these." Chufat flashes his gold teeth.

There's a puzzled buzz, irritated growls.

"Hah?"

"Stop talking foolishness."

"Just because we're pigs, don't take us for idiots."

No one leaves, though, and Chufat elaborates, "Gold teeth would have made me a marked man, and I had nothing, no birthmark or scar, not one distinguishing feature that would let man-catchers identify me."

Again there's a buzz, this time from knowing laughter, hands slapping backs, thighs, and Chufat raises his voice,

"That's not all. I was lucky because my *patron's* house servants were native *indios* and mixed-blood *cholos*—like the
men who work here as loaders and the boatmen who bring
supplies from Pisco."

~

PISCO—A CLUSTER of small, sun-scorched houses and tall
palms on an otherwise barren, rocky coast—is some
twelve miles away by Chufat's estimate, directly opposite
the strip of shale where we diggers drag ourselves at day's
end to wash.

This is the island's one beach, and it is guarded by only
two soldiers. Yet even the boldest among us won't step
beyond the ankle-deep water in which we're permitted. Not
for fear of the waves, which are fierce, but on those occasions a digger has inadvertently overreached while rinsing
a jacket, *both* soldiers, barking like the sea lions swarming
over the rocks, have raised their muskets and shot the digger in his legs, ensuring he was caught and suffered prolonged punishments before he died.

Nestled in the rocks, glistening pools of water beckon.
But sea lions bask on these rocks, and their bared teeth,
long as my fingers, are terrifying. Besides, after fourteen,
sixteen hours' labor, few diggers have the energy for raising their voices above the noisy surf to talk let alone
climbing rocks baked red-hot by the relentless sun.

Indeed, the legs of many diggers fold under them on

arrival at the beach, some before. The rest totter as clumsily as the islands' white-breasted, black-winged birds, the ones I think of as little buffalo because their cries are muted like a buffalo's moan.

Rolling our pants high as they'll go, we make do with dousing ourselves in spray from the waves pummeling the shore. The water, wonderfully cool, turns the guano caked to my skin soapy. But the salt leaves a sticky film, and no matter how hard I scrub my face, arms, legs, and chest with the rag from around my neck, I can't feel clean.

What I do feel is dismay at the numerous arms and backs that are crisscrossed with fresh wounds, old scars, the angry purple and red sores mottling skin. How long can I keep mine unbroken, sealed from infection?

In my exhaustion at day's end, I sometimes lose my balance as receding waves scoop out the shells and stones beneath my feet, and were it not for the thick calluses on my soles, my skin would be punctured as I slip and slide. If I ever fail to break my fall, my legs, back, and arms will surely be pierced; beyond the reach of cooling water, my skin will be seared by the shale's white heat.

More than once, while struggling to regain my balance, yelps have leaped unbidden from my lips. Whenever a buffalo bird peeps, the entire flock responds, twisting their necks and heads from side to side until they locate the source, then waddling and hobbling over as fast as they can, their wings sticking out like short, stiff arms. But at my bleats, diggers near me avert their heads the way I do when others cry or tumble. Whatever strength a digger has is saved for helping brothers, cousins, close friends, lovers. Mine are too far away to hear me, and since we're paid in scrip, I have no means to send them a letter.

In truth, it isn't only that which keeps me from writing but shame. My capture has surely added to my family's burdens. How can I heap more worries on them by revealing my sufferings?

~

THE LAST COCOON reeled, my sisters-in-law, nieces, and I bring out our embroidery frames, silks, and needles for our winter work.

This is the season for visiting. But we still have no word from Ah Lung, and villagers, afraid our bad luck will infect them, avoid us the way they would a family in mourning.

I am not afraid that Ah Lung is dead. If he were, my heart would know it. But he must be suffering, otherwise he'd write. Aching with worry, I ask, "Husband, where are you? Are you suffering because there are no free Chinese near? I know from your sister that your contract cannot be broken. Given the means, though, could a free Chinese buy your freedom? Is there one who would?"

Bᴏᴀᴛᴍᴇɴ ғʀᴏᴍ Pɪsᴄᴏ deliver barrels of water and food daily. These supplies are for everybody on the island: five-hundred diggers, fifty drivers, one-hundred loaders, and the devil-king. But the drivers won't carry barrels from the beach to the storage sheds any more than the devil-king, and there are too many ships waiting for guano to spare loaders for the chore. So when the Pisco boat is forty, fifty feet from the island, devil-drivers choose a half-dozen of the strongest diggers and order them to the beach.

The distance between beach and sheds is a half-mile. Many trips are required. And since carrying the barrels does not excuse a digger from meeting his daily quota of guano, I'm impatient when, raising my hands over my eyes to shield them from the glare, I see the boat bobbing on kingfisher-blue swells like a seabird at rest.

At the same time, I realize the boat is where the swells begin heaving in ever steeper slopes, becoming the waves that crash against the rocks, this scrap of beach, and from maneuvering our family's skiff in rough water, I know any boat attempting to rush in would swamp.

The boatmen from Pisco never hurry. Alternately resting and riding the rollers, they edge closer, then dart through the breakers in a final spurt that always lands them safely on the beach.

I believe Chufat was similarly masterful in handling his escape from the plantation.

⁓

PASSING THE DEVIL-*patron's* house while walking back and forth from the sleeping sheds to the cane fields or the sugar mill, Chufat had noted the open cooking shed at the end of a breezeway, the side yard where the servants hung their own freshly washed clothes to dry. One by one and with months in between so as to avoid notice, Chufat stole a small, sharp knife, pair of white pants, shabby hat, patched shirt, and well worn hemp sandals, hid each item in his bedding.

He picked up Spanish words by eavesdropping on the servants, listening closely to the devil-*patron* and the devil-drivers, matching the interpreter's translations to what they'd said. When protected by the din of the sugar mill, Chufat practiced saying the Spanish words out loud. Locked in for the night, he kept to himself. Discreetly studying the sleeping shed's cane walls, he silently reviewed his expanding vocabulary, arranged and rearranged the words into sentences:

Un plan, a plan.

Necesito, I need.

Tengo, I have.

Necesito un plan.

Tengo un plan.

⁓

BACK IN THE close quarters of the devil-ship's between-decks, talk was such a constant that I came to understand words from other dialects without making the smallest effort. Then, too, if I was slow rising from all fours at the cookhouse and a devil, pricking my neck with the point of his bayonet, snapped, *"Hurry,"* the meaning was clear. When Red barked, "Joe," and a sailor whose skin gleamed like the finest black lacquer appeared, that had to be his name.

Yet I didn't pick up any English beyond commands and names. While under the watchful eyes of the captain and Red, the crew didn't, so far as I could determine, ever break the rule forbidding them to converse amongst themselves when on duty. And, with the exception of Joe, sailors sent below as guards protected themselves from the awful reek by tying cloths over their noses and mouths. To maintain order, they relied entirely on their bayonets' sharp blades to speak for them.

There were times I could have sworn that Joe and Ah Ming were talking to each other. But whenever I cocked an ear for confirmation or shifted a little to see, Ah Ming would be making a remark to someone else; Joe would be nowhere near.

I could have questioned Ah Ming directly. Just as I could have asked him to teach me more English. Much as he might have scoffed, which I dreaded, he'd have obliged. He might even have taken me into his confidence. But I did not then understand what could be gained by knowing the language of our captors.

Now that I do, I wonder whether Ah Ming really was suffering the agonies of cholera when Joe hauled him, groaning, above or if the two were enacting a plan plotted in secret; for later that same day, the cooks issued hard biscuits and plain water in place of rice, then the hatch grating slammed shut and its bolts rasped, signifying the ship was headed into a port. So Ah Ming, once out of our hearing, might well have turned silent, and Joe, instead of carrying him to the sickroom, might have pretended he was already dead, thrown him overboard with weights deliberately knotted to fall away. Ah Ming could then have swum to another vessel or to shore and returned home.

$\backsim$

IF THERE IS a digger on this dunghill who knows Spanish, I have not come across him. Nor does the devil-king employ either servants or an interpreter. Every unfortunate here is his servant, and he has no need for an interpreter since experienced diggers easily cover the essentials for new arrivals and the devil-drivers work us with their whips rather than their tongues.

During our daily meal break, the drivers flock together and chatter like raucous magpies, providing ample opportunities for eavesdropping. But by the time they call the break, we've been digging, shoveling, and delivering guano to the depot for six hours straight. Long after every digger has dropped his tools, I feel the repeated stabs of pickaxes from the soles of my feet to my skull, the muscles in my arms and legs twitch, sweat still streams from my every pore, and I am incapable of anything beyond falling on my meager ration of tepid tea and rancid goat meat in a mess of rice and beans.

As for the loaders, the closest I get to them is at the depot, a large area near the edge of a cliff that is enclosed by a wall of stout cane.

PLUMES OF GUANO dust leap above the depot's wall like flames. As I approach, I stop a moment, take the rag from my neck and wrap it around my head so it covers my nose and mouth. Before stepping through the break in the wall that serves as the depot's entrance, I narrow my eyes.

Instantly, I'm shrouded in a yellow fog. Dark shadows

loom. Lithe black snakes hiss warnings, strike flesh. Howls are frequent as bird cries, the rumble of wheelbarrows, the pounding surf.

Feeling as if I've crossed the Yellow River into Hell, I bawl out my number to the burly shadow responsible for keeping tally of our loads, *"Cuatro!"*

Back home, we always avoided the number four since sei has the same sound as death. On this dunghill, the number is doubly cursed because it belonged to a digger now dead. True, every digger bears a dead man's number, and *cuatro* doesn't sound remotely like sei. Still a shiver chills my spine each time I give my number, and I offer up a quick prayer for mercy.

Mercy. The driver tallying loads could, on seeing a digger stagger through the entrance, show mercy by making two or even three checkmarks next to the digger's number instead of one. Who would see him perform this kindness? How would the devil-king find out and fault him? Yet no digger, to my knowledge, has enjoyed any such benevolence from a driver. Certainly I have not.

Like every digger though, I've had to swallow the injustice of a driver declaring my load short, I've suffered the misery of making it up. So when the burly shadow raises an arm in acceptance and waves me on, I'm relieved.

Lurching forward, my gut tightens. Already I'm wheezing and grunting for breath under my cloth muzzle, blundering because I instinctively keep sealing my eyes against the hurtful dust, and before I can pitch out my load, I must descend a steep slope.

The ground here, covered with drifts of loose guano, is treacherous: One leg can sink as far as the ankle or calf, the other up to the knee. Fighting to keep a heavy wheelbarrow from becoming a runaway, my muscles strain and cramp; my arms threaten to yank out of their sockets. Doubled over from a basket of guano on my back, I stumble more frequently, bumping into other diggers.

More than once, I've come close to being buried in a headlong tumble. Even when I feel my limbs, all atremble, cannot be trusted, however, I don't ditch my load sooner than I should. To be a lucky runaway like Chufat, I must remain unmarked, and devil-drivers, despite the blinding dust, manage to catch miscreants with their whips.

SHIPS COMING FOR guano anchor on the depot side of the island where there is little wind. While the sea around the anchorage is undisturbed by a single ripple, surf dashes against the dunghill's rocks in sheets fifty feet high, sometimes more, and at the cliff's edge, where we're supposed to dump our guano, the noise is deafening.

Such strong surf makes it impossible for ships to get any closer to the island than thirty or forty yards. So loaders in the depot shovel the guano into chutes of wood and canvas, each as large as an oversized barrel and sufficiently long to reach beyond the rocks, the worst of the surf.

When emptying my basket or wheelbarrow, I'm less than ten feet from these loaders. But there's almost as much guano in the air as on the ground, and the only way I can distinguish loaders from diggers is by the flash of their shovels slicing through the murk, their muffled summons for us to come close:

"Venga aquí!"

"Aquí!"

"Aquí!"

Eᴠᴇʀʏ ᴅᴀʏ, ᴀs the blood-red sun sinks into the sea, devil-drivers thunder, *"Venga aquí,"* from the doors of our sleeping sheds. Since laggards are rewarded with the lash, I hurry as best I can to obey.

Inside, perfumed incense from a small shrine mingles with the stink of guano. Some diggers, too exhausted to plod down to the beach to wash, already lie senseless on their beds. There are also beds that will stay empty, their occupants struggling to fulfill their quotas or under punishment or dead. The rest of us shuffle through the slivers of space between beds until we reach our own, collapse, sit, squat, or stretch out, light our pipes.

The sheds housing loaders and drivers are as ramshackle as ours. Their doors, however, have no bolts on the outside to lock them in, and despite the huge stretches of hard-packed guano separating our ten sheds from the loaders' two and the drivers' one, delicious aromas from their outdoor cooking fires soon filter in, spurring many a digger to pull his blanket over his face. But the shed is still baking from the day's heat; the foreign wool is scratchy and harbors fleas that suck our blood as greedily as the devils. So I blot out the smells the same way I smother my hunger—by puffing harder on my pipe, returning to Chufat's escape from the plantation.

CHUFAT CHOSE A night when no moon silvered the cracks in his sleeping shed's walls. Faking sleep, he waited until the rowdy gaming stopped, talking dwindled into the occasional murmur, faded into silence, and no fresh pipesmoke threaded the shed's stale air. Then he burrowed under his blanket and, making as few movements as possible, undressed, hacked off his queue, wrapped and knotted it around his jacket and pants, creating a compact bundle he could bury beyond the cane fields. Just as carefully, he slipped on his stolen clothing, rolled over onto his belly. Finally, he sliced through the vines binding the lengths of cane that formed the wall behind his bed, seized the bundle he'd made, and slid out.

Invariably, Chufat pauses here when telling his story, beckons the *indio* or mixed-blood *cholo* who has rowed him over from North Island and is squatting nearby. In a few strides, the boatman is standing beside Chufat, and it has been my observation that the *indios* have generally been

darker, shorter, and more square than Chufat, while *cholos*
have often had higher noses, more facial hair, and round-
er eyes. But there's always enough of a resemblance in col-
oring, build, and features between boatman and merchant
that no digger has ever disputed Chufat's boast: "Not one
man-catcher gave me a second glance."

Many diggers, especially those who were decoyed by
relatives or friends, have difficulty believing Chufat wasn't
turned in for a reward by any of the *indios* or *cholos* from
whom he sought food and shelter, those who gave him
refuge. When these diggers say as much, Chufat retorts,
"Had I been betrayed, I'd either be cutting cane or dead."

True. Unless Chufat was never a pig and is pretending
in order to ingratiate himself, to win our admiration and
respect. After all, we know from his tireless tongue that in
Peru's capital, Lima, there is a colony of free Chinese large
enough to have merchant guilds, and even in small towns,
there are emigrants from Gold Mountain as well as home
who come because of the money that can be made from
running stores, restaurants, and rooming houses. There
are also former pigs: Most were cast adrift by their masters
after they became too broken for hard labor, but some
survived harsh periods of indenture without breaking, or
had the rare honest and fair master, or are successful run-
aways. Chufat could have borrowed his story whole or in
bits and pieces from them.

Regardless, it's clear that had I slumped on the deck of

the devil-ship as if I were too weak to stand, I'd have landed in a fatteninghouse on the mainland from which I could have escaped, then found work among Callao's Chinese and begun earning silver instead of scrip.

Can I apply Chufat's plan here?

OUR SLEEPING SHEDS are so poorly built that the weakest among us could wedge an opening between planks with his bare hands and slither out.

But the devil-king—relying on brokers in Callao to supply him with diggers—never leaves this island, and his palace, situated on an outcrop of rock, overlooks the beach, the depot, the ships at anchor, all traffic between the moorings, islands, and mainland, ensuring no one sets foot on or off this island except on his authority.

Devil though he be, however, the king surely has to sleep, and I doubt he can see in the dark. So on a moonless night, couldn't a digger slip past him and any guards he's posted?

Yes!

But starting in the late afternoon, the beach and every rock surrounding the island, indeed most of the dunghill, is taken over by thousands of birds and sea lions settling for the night, making it impossible for anyone to reach water without going through them, raising a ruckus that would bring the devils running.

Then again, wouldn't my flight be hidden by hundreds, thousands of birds taking wing?

Of course!

And I'd be as certain to topple over a cliff's edge as a deliberate suicide.

~

FEW DAYS PASS without a digger ending his misery by making a dash for a cliff's edge, then leaping off. No matter where these suicides jump, they don't land in water, but upon the jagged rocks below. Few die immediately, and despite their howls, vultures swoop down to tear at their flesh until the surf drags their remains into the sea.

Diggers who die chained to the punishment rock or skiff are similarly devoured. But those who fail to wake in the morning or die under the lash are buried in shallow graves at day's end by the first diggers to meet their quotas.

"Three years is the life expectancy of a digger," Chufat says, pulling his face long as a mourner's. "And there's no hope of escape for a digger like there is for pigs on the mainland. That's why I'm willing to sacrifice my own comfort for yours."

Elaborating on these sacrifices, Chufat likes to dwell on how desirable *india, chola,* and black women find Chinese men because of their enterprise, the money they make.

"I can assure you from experience that the women are

desirable, too. Why else would most former pigs choose to settle here instead of going home?"

Whether the women in Peru are desirable, I do not care. I only want Bo See. But I can see from the varied features, hair, and shades of skin color on drivers as well as boatmen that there is much mixing among different peoples, and Chufat has, over time, described in vivid detail more than one woman in Pisco on whom he's set his sights.

Always he concludes, "With the losses I'm suffering on your account, what woman will want me? I'll be lucky if I don't have to sell my gold teeth one by one."

Once, a burly fellow a few feet from Chufat made a fist and shook it at him, saying, "You'll be lucky if I don't knock out the lot to make up for what you're stealing from us!"

"You know I'm not the thief. As for my being lucky, haven't you heard me make that claim myself?" Chufat offered the threatener a lump of rock sugar. "And by sweetening your misery, I'm sharing some of that luck with you."

How far would he be willing to extend himself in sharing that luck, I wonder.

⁓

I WAIT UNTIL Chufat's sold everything he's brought and we are alone except for his helper, who's piling up empty baskets.

Then, sidling close, I feel Chufat out by asking for goods he's never had: paper, brush, inkstick, and inkstone.

"Here," he says, tearing the used pages from his red-covered account book.

He tips his head in the direction of his brush, inkstick, and inkstone. "You can have those as well, and seeing as how none of these items are new, I'll even give you a discount."

The man would probably sell every stitch of the clothing he's wearing were there money to be made from it. So as I take scrip from my pocket, I continue in a plaintive tone, "I'd like to write my fam—"

Breaking in, Chufat reminds me that the boat which brings him from North Island ties up in a sheltered cove directly below the devil-king's palace. Then he and his boatman have to carry his baskets and bundles up a series of flimsy ladders that creak and rattle against the craggy cliff face. Landing on the beach would be easier. Safer. But the devil-king would have to descend from his palace or rely on others to match the scrip turned in against the merchandise landed, and the devil forbids it.

"Really, I'm at the devil's mercy almost as much as you," he finishes, deftly plucking all six pieces of scrip from my hand.

His cloaked refusal isn't a surprise. Yet disappointment swells. Hoping I can turn him around through flattery, I fawn, "Master Chufat, you know *everything*. Should the envelope have Canton, China in Spanish—"

He cuts me off with a harsh, "Dui! I'll speak plain. I won't send a letter for you."

Under his angry outburst, hope shrivels. Clearly Chufat would never risk his skin to save mine.

IN THE SLEEPING shed, I drop my purchases, myself onto my bed. At each thump, there's a puff of guano dust flecked with fleas. Spiders and small lizards that have been hiding under my blanket scurry out, disappear.

From the bed to my left, Ah Kam's arm shoots over and snags my book. "You've not stolen Chufat's accounts have you?" Riffling the pages, he sees they're blank, jeers, "I didn't think you were the daring type." He eyes the brush, inkstick, and inkstone. "What are you going to write? Chufat's story? You've certainly listened to him often enough to have it memorized."

Men in nearby beds snort, guffaw.

"Nah. He's going to write to our devil-king."

"What? Ask for better food?"

"Reduced loads?"

"Freedom! He's going to petition for our freedom."

"Wah, our very own Fook Sing Gung."

Their banter underscores my defeat, and I curl up like a baby, the baby Bo See and I might have made together but didn't.

NIGHT AFTER NIGHT, whether I am staring into darkness or have stumbled at last into thin, fitful sleep, my arms sweep the bedmat for Ah Lung—only to embrace air.

Neither of us had been in a hurry to share our bed with a baby, to give up the freedom of reaching for each other whenever our blood thickened with desire. Now, lying alone, I mourn the seed we used to deliberately waste; my fingers trace the shapes of babies on my belly.

Finally, I quit bed and sleeping room for the wormhouse. On the shelves are dozens of small squares of paper, each with five-hundred eggs the size of fly specks. Naturally sticky, the eggs hold fast to the papers, and I bind these eggsheets to my chest and belly and back with a long cloth.

Encased in eggsheets, I am careful not to splash while drawing water from the village well. I try not to bend so I won't crumple the paper. I will myself not to hurry despite the whispers of women and girls waiting their turns.

"Bo See's been looking like a ghost. Now she's turned stiff as wood."

"Didn't I say she'd lose her self-control and go mad from grief?"

"You weren't the only one to make that prediction."

"And no wonder! Have you ever heard of a pig returning?"

"I'll wager Ah Lung is dead."

"I blame Bo See. Remember how she tumbled out of her bridal sedan?"

"You think *that* is the reason for the Wongs' misfortune?"

"Yeah."

"Maybe. Don't you pity Bo See anyway?"

"Because she's so young a widow?"

"A *childless* widow."

"She could take a child to raise as her own."

"Don't be absurd! How can a madwoman be a mother?"

WHILE WAITING FOR their cargo, those on board the guano ships must endure the same relentless stink and heat we do. During loading, they're swathed in yellow clouds of dust as thick and choking as the worst we suffer. Not surprisingly, the moment the last shovelful is in, the hatches battened down, the decks washed clean, the sailors on the lucky ship hoist their national flag, then light torches.

Watching them, listening to the sailors cheer and the crews on the other vessels respond in kind, I always erupt in envy. Even after we're locked in for the night, I cannot stop myself from staring through the gaps between planks in the wall facing the sea, the flashes of red, blue, and yellow from the rockets and flares set off in celebration. And when the devil-drivers release us at dawn, my heart wrenches at the unmistakable clack-clack of anchor chains, the sound of sailors chanting to its beat.

The mist is too dense for me to see further than a few feet, but I imagine myself on board the ship: Its anchor raised, its sails unfurl; wind whistles through the rigging, filling the canvas; the prow cuts through the sea, flinging back great wings of water. . . .

Devil-drivers bellow, shattering my dream. The sailors' song fades. There is only the sound of the surf, diggers cursing, hawking spit, the clatter of our pickaxes, shovels, screens, and wheelbarrows.

Through the thinning mist, the ships at anchor look like a mysterious village under leafless trees, and the stretch of water between dunghill and anchorage is too great for me to ever clearly see the people on board. If the surf is low and the sea lions and birds have not wakened yet, however, I sometimes hear voices. Not just of men, but women and children.

This morning, a woman's angry shrill is swiftly followed by a child's shriek, and I am reminded of Old Lady Chow, our near neighbor in Strongworm when I was a boy, swooping me up like a hawk, my instant and fierce resistance.

A whip cracks. I pick up my pace, sense a general quickening in our ranks. How well schooled in obedience we've become in our captivity!

No, not in captivity. Not me. Since proper order demanded my parents punish me for resisting Old Lady Chow, any elder, including my brothers, I long ago learned unquestioning obedience, and it cost me my natural wit and courage, then my family.

⁓

AFTER I RETURN home with the day's water, Ma lights incense. The family bows and prays for Heaven's protection, for a letter from Ah Lung, for proof he's alive. I edge away from the altar so the fragrant smoke can't seep through my clothing and taint the eggs.

Second Sister-in-law plucks my sleeve. "Bo See, are you unwell?"

I snatch for an acceptable excuse. "A little faint."

"Sit down. I'll bring you some white flower oil."

Alarmed at the injury such a pungent oil would inflict, I grip Second Sister-in-law's arm.

"It's not necessary."

The others notice, fuss.

"Go lie down," Ma urges.

That, though, would crush the eggs on my back and, mumbling it's fresh air I need, I dodge out the front door.

⁓

IN THE SLEEPING shed, some of the stronger men gather and, using scrip, the promise of future rations, a load towards the next day's quota, place wagers on games of dominoes, fan tan, checkers. Fragrances drifting in with smoke from the drivers' cooking fires loosen the tongues of men sprawled in their beds.

"They're stewing the pigs' feet I hauled up from the beach this morning."

"Nah, it's that fatty porkback."

"Yeah, fatty porkback fried with spicy peppers."

"Corn, too."

"Mmmm, roasting in the fires' wood ash."

My need growing greater than my shame, I flatten my palms on my bedboards, ease my knees down onto the narrow strip of guano floor between beds, fumble for my manhood, and wet the inkstone's shallow depression with a splash of piss, then grind my inkstick into it as I would a pestle and mortar.

Little light reaches me from the lantern over the gamblers, but it is enough. Opening Chufat's book, I dip my brush into the ink and pour out my anguish.

"Let's tell our Fook Sing Gung the dishes we want cooked for us from now on," Ah Kam suggests. "I'll take roasted sweet potatoes."

"Give me the webbing on duck's feet."

"That's good and chewy alright."

"Honey-sweet, yet salty."

Behind me, bedboards creak. Moments later, my light is blocked by Ah Kam leaning over my shoulder.

"Too bad we can't eat the chicken intestines you're producing."

Recoiling from his invasion, his sour breath, I dip my head closer to the paper, shielding the rows of characters, my nose.

"Aw, what a shy bride," he teases.

"Bride? He's supposed to be our God of Luck."

"Maybe he's a lucky bride."

"Alas, no." Ah Kam snatches the book, reads in a mocking tone:

"Savages have taken me prisoner.

I strain my eyes

Looking for my dear ones,

But my dear ones do not appear.

I . . ."

He chokes to a halt. No one scoffs or teases. Gently, one man urges him on, then another. And when Ah Kam does take up where he broke off, it is clear he is lamenting from his heart.

"I strain my ears

Listening for my dear ones,

But I do not hear their voices.

Alone among strangers and barbarians,

My sorrow is bigger than a mountain,

My tears fall like rain."

As Ah Kam chants, the gamblers stop their play; every man in the shed falls silent. Even after Ah Kam, head bowed, closes the book, the only sounds are ragged breaths, stifled sobs.

The lantern sputters, dims. Still no man speaks. But I hear Moongirl high, clear, and insistent:

"By clever planning,

You *can* turn your situation around."

ALL MY ATTENTION directed at keeping safe the eggs against my skin, I become careless with my needle, stab my finger. At the sharp prick, I thrust the injured finger into my mouth—and my eyes flood at the memory of Ah Lung tearing the button from his jacket for me to stitch, my hand sliding across his naked chest.

My heart flutters.

No, not my heart.

Nor is that fluttering but the faint scritch-scratch of newly-hatched worms, and I shiver with the same joyful wonder as a mother at her baby stirring within.

IN MY SLEEP, I reach for Bo See. Instead of warm flesh, my fingers close over something hard, and I startle awake clutching Chufat's account book with this thought: The devil-king cannot command the Pisco boatmen as he does Chufat. Not while the devil is dependent on the food and water the boatmen bring. Which is to say, not ever.

Uncertain what to make of this revelation, I stare into the smoky darkness of the shed. Traces of cool, salt- and guano-laden mist slither through cracks in the walls, and my skin prickles with goosebumps.

Beds creak; shadows shift as men burrow further under their blankets. Hoping the cold will sharpen my mind, I kick mine away—and I am rewarded with the memory of how Moongirl, in making her move from Strongworm to Canton, sought the help of friends.

Can I befriend the Pisco boatmen?

At the attention that would draw on myself, the suspicions I might arouse, the punishment I could then suffer, my breath catches.

"I didn't think you were the daring type."

Ah Kam's jeer, snaking into my head, cuts deep as a driver's lash. The men's derisive calls for me to be their Fook Sing Gung slice like the weighted cords of the devil-captain's punishment whip, and I have to fold my lips to keep from crying out.

Fear didn't stop me from joining in the mutiny, though. Neither will fear stop me from seeking escape through the Pisco boatmen.

But first I need a plan.

As IDEAS COME to me, I examine them for practicality. One by one, I discard the impossible, expand the attainable.

Then I search Chufat's plan for strategies that should be retained.

Assembling the result, I shuffle the steps, refine them.

Finally, I am ready to begin.

I LONG AGO acquired the ability to sense the boatmen's impending arrival by the intensity of the sun's heat, my craving for water, rest. Then I'd keep my head low so I could better evade the attention of a devil-driver, the order to go to the beach.

Today, I deliberately raise my head, turn it as if loosening the stiffness in my neck.

Almost at once, a driver snaps, *"Vete a la playa."*

Disguising my eagerness in a groveling bow, I obey.

As usual, the drivers have ordered six of us to the beach. On our way, we have each picked up a yoke and two empty barrels from the storage sheds. We've stacked the twelve barrels to create a small shaded area in which we squat after rinsing the rags from around our necks, washing off the guano coating our faces.

My heart drumming wildly, I study the rollers that will bring in the boat and are yet empty, muttering, "Those devils order us down early just so it'll be tougher for us to make up the time lost."

"I was already behind."

"Me, too."

"That's why the devils picked us!"

Every voice is, like mine, cracked from thirst, all but smothered by the raucous birdcalls and pounding surf. Lest talk fade entirely, I give it a stir.

"I tell you, when you're unlucky, *nothing* goes well. Even water will catch between your teeth."

"Water I'd welcome."

"Good well water, not the foul stuff from Pisco."

My eyes trained on the rollers, I return to the difficulty of meeting our quotas. "Maybe we could make up some time by helping to haul in the boat."

"And squander what little strength we have?"

"Where's the gain in that?"

"Are you crazy?"

I both expected and desired their reluctance. But their concerns reflect my own, and I have to bolster my wavering resolve before I can stammer, "It's worth a try."

At this same moment, the boat's prow appears, and I stagger to my feet.

"You really have gone mad."

"You'll be shot."

This warning has reared up in me already, and although I again assure myself that the soldiers have never troubled anyone who stays well within the shallows, my heart thrashes madly against my chest, my toes curl into the shale as I wait for the boat to make its final dart through the breakers, to cross into where we're permitted.

By then, the boatmen have leaped into the water; instead I've half-buried my feet, and my legs have turned to lead. Somehow, though, I lift one foot, then the other, and, despite angry barks from the soldiers, stumble into water, hurl myself against the side of the boat, help drag it in.

EVER SINCE CHUFAT opened my eyes to the importance of knowing Spanish, I have been looking for meaning in the bits of jibber-jabber I catch through repetition. Because he and his boatmen acknowledge drivers and loaders with "*Buenas tardes*," while the Pisco boatmen and soldiers call out, "*Buenos días*," upon arrival, I have decided these must be greetings: the former for afternoon, the latter for morning. Similarly, the exchanges of "*adiós*," at partings must be "farewell;" the "*gracias*" offered each time someone accepts a smoke or a light must be an expression of thanks, the response, "*de nada*," akin to "no thanks are necessary." So when the Pisco boatmen belt a hearty chorus of "*gracias*" for my help, I try to come back with "*de nada*." But my tongue, sliding across the roof of my mouth, strikes teeth, and my jaw, clenched tight, refuses to open.

Even after the soldiers stop barking, lower their muskets,

and start exchanging greetings with the boatmen as usual, I cannot pry loose my jaw. So I cannot defend myself against the diggers swarming across the beach, buzzing and stinging.

"What a fool!"

"You could have brought trouble on us all."

"You nearly did!"

Willing my features into the serene mask that Bo See always presented to her abusers, I dodge past them to fetch a yoke, trot back, and attach a pair of barrels the boatmen have unloaded.

The next time I help bring in the boat, the soldiers and diggers again snap and snarl, rendering me incapable of speech. Little by little, however, their loud rebukes diminish into scowls, and I manage to address the boatmen.

Then I realize boatmen and soldiers sometimes attach what seem like names to their greetings and farewells. So I start studying faces.

Finally, I match "Miguel" with the most heavily stubbled jaw, and after I hail him by name, he gestures for me to share mine.

Now the four call out, "*Buenos días*, Ah Lung," as I jog toward their boat, and I can recognize "Luis" by his squashed nose and distinctive waddle; "Roberto" by his wide, flat face; and "Alfonso" by his winglike ears, his lips pursed for whistling.

If only snatching meaning from their rivers of talk were as straightforward!

Mi. Me? My?

Casa. House.

Mi casa. Home?

⁓

THE RUMBLE IN Ba's chest has deepened with winter. Ma leans ever more heavily on my sisters-in-law and myself when we help her shift from bed to chair or hobble to the family altar. Yet their concern is not for themselves but their missing son. Indeed, Ah Lung's silence weighs on the whole family. After Moongirl writes that she has a new client whose husband, Master Yee, ships goods to Chinese merchants in Peru, however, our spirits rise.

A thousand times a day I repeat Moongirl's words to myself, "Master Yee has sent a letter to the merchants' guild asking them to look for Ah Lung."

Now, hoisting Ba up in his bed and giving him his orange-rind brew, I ask, "Would the merchants' guild have the power to secure Ah Lung's freedom?"

"You mean to buy out his contract?"

Despite the sunlight beaming across the bed, Ba is ashen, his grip on the steaming-hot bowl so desperate I fear he's chilled, and I take a second padded jacket from the nail behind the door, drape it over his shoulders.

"Power lies in money. So the merchants' guild undoubtedly *does* have the power to buy Ah Lung's freedom. But the price would be high, very high, and Moongirl's fallen into debt from all the extra expenses since Ah Lung's capture."

My heart thumping, I say, "We can increase our worm and leaf production."

Ba sighs. "You know a family can't raise more worms than there are hands to care for them, and we're stretched to the limit."

"For each generation of worms that we raise, yes. But we can add an eighth generation."

"Impossible!"

His dismissal, though, is thick with longing, and as I help him guide the bowl to his lips, I lay out my plan.

"By incubating the eggs on our bodies, we can hasten their hatching by three-and-a-half days. Come summer's heat, the eggs are bound to hatch even faster, and the accumulated time saved will allow us to raise an eighth generation before the weather turns too cool."

My plan unfolded, I feel as if I have stepped into the calm of the wormhouse, and my head is clear, my heartbeat steady as Ba takes a final gurgling swallow, then surrenders the empty bowl.

"How can you be so certain?"

"I tried it."

"That's why you were avoiding the altar and moving stiffly!"

"Yes."

"You're not yourself or you'd realize you can't work moving that awkwardly, *and* you'd injure whatever worms you didn't lose or kill during a transfer from bodies to trays."

"The moths can lay eggs on squares of cloth. Then we'll be able to move freely. And we'll remove the eggcloths from our bodies just before the eggs are due to hatch."

Ba's breath quickens, and he leans forward. "How will we feed an eighth generation?"

"Instead of waiting until the end of the silk season to drain the fishponds and dig up the mud, do it while we're raising the seventh generation of worms, then pile the mud around the base of each mulberry shrub to force an eighth crop."

"You're right!" he exults. "We *can* increase both our worm and leaf production! We *will!*"

"For you," I tell Ah Lung. "For you."

WHEN I CLIMB onto the boat to get barrels for my yoke
instead of waiting for the boatmen to unload them, I'm
ignored by soldiers and diggers. I'd even wager I've
become as invisible to them as Joe and Ah Ming were to
the crew and piggies on the devil-ship. But I take no
chances. When I attempt boarding the boat from different
approaches, I imitate the techniques of a boxing master
who disarms opponents by skipping with back rounded,
shoulders relaxed, hands hooked, and eyes alert like a
monkey. Whenever I snatch a boatman's hat and plop it
onto my head for a moment or two before returning it, I
chitter and frolic, scuffing up bits of shale, splatters of
water.

Careful not to prolong my play or go deeper than we're
permitted, I arouse no reaction beyond the ready laughter
of the boatmen. I become adept at leaping from beach to
deck. I discover Roberto's hat best for hiding the queue

coiled around my crown, shielding my face from view. I don't just help haul in the boat but labor alongside the boatmen pushing it back into the sea.

At night, I crawl under my blanket as if to shut out the fragrances from the drivers' cooking fires. Then, as greedily as a miser fingering his coins, I curl my tongue around the small horde of Spanish words I've gleaned, lingering over those that taste especially sweet:

Amigo, friend.

Por favor, please.

Deseo, I want.

Ayúdame, help me.

Esposa, wife.

I find ways to give these words voice so I can confirm my understanding, discover whether I can make myself understood to the Pisco boatmen.

On board their boat, I grunt, *"Ayúdame, por favor,"* while lifting a barrel.

No boatman responds.

Hoping it's because I've been drowned out by the noise from the surf, barrels rolling across the deck and thudding against the boat's side, and the bottom of the hull crunching into shale, I raise my voice. *"Ayúdame, por favor."*

Still no boatman comes to my aid.

So I fall back on the familiar, *"Venga aquí."*

As Miguel hurries over, I add, *"Ayúdame, por favor."*

Miguel cocks his head in puzzlement.

Grasping the barrel with both hands, I signal my need for help with an exaggerated groan.

Amused understanding flashes across his face, and he says, *"Ayúdame, por favor,"* but very differently from my garblings.

I imitate the way he shapes his lips, change how I place my tongue. *"Ayúdame, por favor."*

Miguel shakes his head. *"A-yú-da-me, por favor."*

I echo him.

He gestures for me to run the sounds together.

I repeat, *"Ayúdame, por favor."*

He beams approval. *"Bueno."*

⌒

CERTAIN, NOW, THAT I'll be understood, I sing, "Roberto, *mi amigo*," and point to his hat perched on my head. *"Deseo."*

He mimes for me to keep it.

Clamping the hat down so it conceals my queue and shadows my face, I bow deeply. *"Gracias."*

He throws an arm over my shoulder. *"De nada, mi amigo."*

His unhesitating generosity and confirmation of friendship are, I tell myself, good omens. Even so, my innards cramp and twist as I trot beside him to the boat, then slip in front of Alfonso, who is whistling a joyful tune, seize the rough, sun-warm wood, push.

"Aarrrgh!"

At the anguished wail from a digger shackled to the punishment rock, my chest tightens as does my grip; my legs turn to rubber. But Alfonso doesn't miss a note, and I maintain the rhythmic slap-slap of my feet with the boatmen's.

As we push past ankle deep water, I forge forward instead of falling back. The moment the bottom of the boat stops rasping against shale, I leap on board with the boatmen.

Dropping onto my knees, I clap my hands together, panting, "*Amigo, ayúdame! Deseo mi esposa. Necesito mi esposa, mi casa. Ayúdame, por favor—*"

My chin strikes wood; I bite my tongue. Reeling from the pain, I'm uncertain whether I've been knocked flat by a boatman, if the boat is yet rolling from shore or now catching a wave that will take me back.

Then cries of "*adiós*" fly between the boatmen and the soldiers, and the tightness in my chest eases: The boatmen will not betray me; nor have the soldiers noticed my absence, which means no alarm will be raised. For the desperation of diggers to avoid punishment makes it unnecessary for devil-drivers to mark their return from the beach. Indeed, the devils only make a count of diggers when calculating how many replacements are needed, and there's never any search for the missing. Not even by diggers. When my bed is empty tonight, a few diggers in the sleeping shed might speculate over the cause: Has Ah

Lung failed to meet his quota, been sent for punishment, or thrown himself off a cliff? When my bed stays empty, they'll assume I'm dead.

Spray, cool and cleansing, sprinkles my guano-crusted back, my matted hair.

Hair?

Roberto's hat must have fallen from my head!

I jerk up to look for it. Alfonso, shrilling babble, hits the side of my head in a stinging slap, knees the small of my back, pinning me to the deck.

Have I misjudged the boatmen?

Fingers strong as iron squeeze my shoulder. Their grip, though, is strangely calming. Could Alfonso, still streaming words to which I can attach no meaning, be offering reassurance?

His tone, I realize, is no longer sharp. Rather, it seems warm, cautionary. Could he be warning me?

Yes. Of course!

"*Sí*," I gush. "*Comprendo*."

"*Bueno*, Ah Lung, *mi amigo*."

The relief in Alfonso's voice is almost as great as in mine, and as he releases me, we both sputter nervous laughter. Even without Alfonso's restraining hand, however, I would not have raised my head high enough to be seen. I require no warning to stay hidden.

Sailors rowing skiffs from the guano ships dot these waters, and according to Chufat, the devil-king doesn't just decree the time a guano ship has to wait for loading but whether it is loaded under a chute, which takes three days, or at its moorings, which requires a month. So the very day a ship drops anchor, its captain seeks preferment in loading by calling on the devil-king with gifts of wine and foreign delicacies. From the devil-king's palace, these captains cannot fail to witness the horrific conditions under which diggers are forced to toil, the terrible punishments they suffer. Still, the captains keep bringing their ships for the guano, and I doubt there is one who would hesitate to deliver a digger to the devil-king for preferment.

Then, too, there are fishermen who might, if they catch me, turn me over to the devil for a reward. Certainly I can bring to mind more than one man back in Strongworm who, thrown into the clutches of Old Bloodsucker, would save his family by selling out a stranger, and I'd be surprised if there aren't some as desperate in Pisco. That is why, when making my plan, I determined I'll quit the village immediately after begging a gift of clothes from the boatmen.

Once on the road, I want to believe I'll be as successful as Chufat in eluding notice, then finding work. My difficulty just now in understanding Alfonso, however, is a frightening reminder that Chufat had the advantage of a translator in acquiring his Spanish; he was a pig on the mainland where I have yet to set foot; he has a tongue as quick and honeyed as mine is slow and plain.

Nor have I forgotten how wrong I was in believing we'd won the mutiny on the devil-ship and were homeward bound.

⌐

THE FAMILY HAS worked as one in preventing losses from crushed eggs or strong odors. Each time my sisters-in-law, their older daughters, and I incubate eggs, my brothers-in-law and their older boys perform the household's heavy chores. Ma, reinvigorated by the prospect of securing Ah Lung's freedom, cooks the family's meals with help from Third and Fourth Niece. Ba, propped up in his bed, minds the youngest children.

The village has been no less united and vigorous in ridiculing our efforts. With every generation of eggs that has hatched, however, we've added to the days saved, the certainty of raising an eighth generation of worms, harvesting an extra crop of silk.

"Endure," I beg my husband. "Be patient. Do nothing rash. By season's end we'll have the cash to buy your freedom and purchase your passage home."

⌐

THE SUPPLY BOAT has always come to the dunghill with its barrels of food and water protected by canvas and generous lashings of rope. Before returning to Pisco, the boatmen again cover the empty barrels and tie them down.

Now, as the swells under the boat intensify, signaling land-fall, Luis tugs and yanks off the canvas from the barrels closest to where I'm sprawled on the deck. Miguel squats beside me.

"*Amigo,*" he says, taking one of my hands in his and curling my fingers over a double binding of rope.

Nodding, I grab rope with my other hand too, brace my feet against the boat's side to keep from rolling across the deck and tumbling into the boatmen as they maneuver for landing. Luis and Miguel drag the canvas over me. At their care in covering me from head to toe, poking and tucking in folds so the canvas can't slide off, I realize their intent isn't to protect me from crashing breakers but from prying eyes, and dread, more than the scarcity of air, chokes me.

When the boat shoots forward, I tighten my grip on the ropes and dig my heels into unyielding wood. Hemp bites into my palms. My ankles feel as if they're splintering.

Then the boat is plummeting, bumping my head and knees, scraping my chest across gritty planks. Spray splatters loud as the rapid-fire of lead, skewering the rough canvas to my arms, my back, my legs.

Over and over the boat rides high, then dives; I toss in skin-rending, bone-grinding thumps. Suddenly, though, the skidding and slamming halts; the rat-a-tat of spray above is replaced by the familiar crunch of shale below, and I know we've landed, the boat is being dragged.

In a rush of relief, I let my feet sag onto the deck, tear

my stiffened fingers from the rope. The sections of canvas plastered against me shift. Horrified, I stop.

So does the rattle of shale.

Because the boat is far enough from the water?

Or because my movements have given me away and the boatmen have been ordered to stop?

If there have been any commands, any voices at all, they've been—and are yet—drowned in thundering surf, the blood pounding in my ears. But are those footfalls I feel on the deck?

Yes.

Fighting for calm, I suck in deep breaths of suffocating damp. I remind myself that were we on the dunghill, the boatmen would be reboarding to unload. Likely they follow the same routine here, and the footfalls are theirs.

The thought offers little comfort. Just as I used to help the boatmen unload on the dunghill, there might be villagers who lend a hand here. That could, in fact, be why the boatmen decided to hide me under the canvas.

Perhaps there are even soldiers!

My every nerve and muscle taut, I'm ready to spring to my feet and over the side of the boat while hurling the canvas on top of soldiers aiming muskets, villagers who'd sell me back to the devil-king. But then, in a momentary lull between breakers, I catch Alfonso's joyful whistle threading through the screech and caw of birds. Despite the canvas, I recognize the soothing weight of his hand on my back, clasping my shoulder. So I make no move. Not even after he pulls up the edge of the canvas and I smell woodsmoke in the salt-air.

Yes, the smell of woodsmoke in Strongworm used to send everybody in the fields home, and for as long as we were eating, the streets were empty. But Alfonso must want me to remain hidden or he'd have thrown off the canvas altogether.

⁓

ONCE AGAIN ROBERTO'S straw hat hides my queue, shadows my face. My pants are a gift from Miguel, my shirt from Luis. Of course, my disguise as an *indio* can't shield me from arousing curiosity in Pisco as a stranger, but its huddle of small, poorly plastered houses is far from the water, and although birds are as plentiful in number and variety here as on the dunghill, there don't seem to be any diggers or drivers or soldiers; the boatmen and I are the only people visible on the long, wide beach, the rocks and cliffs beyond.

Gulls and blue, squab-like birds back away from us in beady-eyed huffs, resetting as we pass. Suddenly, there are terrified shrieks and panicked wing flapping not far from the area where we're headed, the area Roberto—smiling and nodding vigorously—pointed to when I told the boatmen I needed work and asked for direction.

Alarmed, I wonder whether Miguel and Luis, going

home to fetch me clothes, slipped in and out in secret or explained what they were doing to their families. If I'm caught, the boatmen's help in my escape will be obvious, so I'm certain I can count on their families' silence even if they don't share the men's willingness to help me. Someone could have overheard Miguel or Luis and decided to set a trap for us, however. Should we run?

Roberto, in the lead, hasn't quickened his pace. Nor have Luis to my right or Miguel to my left. Behind us, Alfonso's whistling is untroubled. Keeping my stride matched to theirs, I try to determine the cause of the disturbance.

Ah!

A short distance from the panicked squawkers, red-throated vultures are hopping jerkily amidst a silent, unmoving mass of black, pouch-beaked birds. From similar scenes I've witnessed, the vultures are probably devouring the gentle pouch-beaked birds' young. Which would mean the other birds aren't squawking and screeching and flapping because men are lurking, setting a trap for the boatmen and myself, but to alert eagles out at sea to the vultures' attack.

I look to the water for confirmation. Sure enough, sea-eagles are beating their wings in a quick return to shore for the babes' defense.

Now, ahead of us, the vultures are taking flight. I know what will happen next. Each of the sea-eagles, flying ever higher, will position itself directly above a vulture. Then the sea-eagle will close its wings and plunge into the vulture with the force of an arrow shot from a bow.

The sea-eagles never miss, and in the fights that follow, the vultures are always mortally wounded. But that doesn't bring the babes back to life or ease their parents' misery any more than it prevents future attacks, and I realize the boatmen's efforts to save me might prove as futile. In truth, although they flank me on every side, I feel as vulnerable as a pouch-beaked babe, and I scour the beach for places from which someone might pounce.

Scattered among the birds and flat-bottomed scows are what look like sheaves of rice. Yet there are no fields in view, nothing growing except scraggly palms. Were the sheaves not commonplace though, wouldn't the boatmen be cocking their heads, muttering to each other in suspicion? And there actually *is* something familiar about the sheaves.

No wonder! They're upturned boats, the kind with tapered prows. While on the dunghill, I saw many such vessels, admired the ease with which they skimmed over the surface of the sea. Chufat called them *caballitos*, little horses, and paddlers straddling these vessels do resemble horsemen. As narrow as these *caballitos* are, however, they're wide enough for a man to hide behind, so I eye them warily.

Then Roberto halts abruptly at a *caballito* that's not upturned to dry but prepared for launching, and I'm grateful beyond measure: The farther I get from Pisco, the safer I'll be, and a *caballito* will carry me away much faster than my feet.

⌐

LUIS, HIS SQUASHED nose flared with emotion, has explained in talk and gestures that he and Miguel will stay in Pisco; we have already exchanged heartfelt farewells. But all four boatmen, standing knee deep in water, hold the *caballito* for me to board. Of course, they cannot prevent the boat, made of reeds, from bobbing in the dangerous swirl of incoming rollers, receding waves, and I fail repeatedly.

When at last I tumble in, I almost swamp the boat. Afraid I'll be knocked back out and, unable to fight the undertow, get dragged to sea while Roberto and Alfonso are boarding, I clutch the sides, dig my fingers deep into the reeds.

Roberto and Alfonso, however, deftly straddle the *caballito* on their first try, and once I'm safely wedged between them, Miguel and Luis release their holds in a final burst of words that are lost in the crashing surf. Then we're hurtling out to sea as if we're galloping over mountains on a well trained horse.

Beyond the breakers, the water—lit by slanting beams of hot afternoon sun—is so clear that I not only see schools of fish flashing gold and silver near the surface but far below. Troops of little black-and-white buffalo birds, absurdly clumsy on land and incapable of flight, deliberately tumble from rocks into the sea with their wings outstretched, turn swift and graceful as they glide into the deep. Giant turtles swim in solitary splendor while sleek, gray snouted creatures—long as I am tall— frolic like children.

Rising from the sea floor is all manner of plant life. The myriad greens are like a glimpse of Strongworm's fields on the other side of the world, and I'm flooded anew with longing for home, gratitude for the boatmen's generosity.

⟋⟍

MOONGIRL SAYS SHIPS take over four months to reach Peru. So the moment Ba approved my plan for incubating eggs and raising an eighth generation of worms, I began urging him to send the merchants' guild a guarantee that we would pay for Ah Lung's freedom, his passage home.

Ba never scolded me for asking, but he insisted, "We should not pledge what we do not have. I'll write soon as we have the cash."

After Ma and Fourth Brother-in-law added their voices to mine, however, Ba surrendered to his own eagerness for Ah Lung's return.

Now, by my calculations, Ba's pledge—turned over to Master Yee through Moongirl, then forwarded to the merchants' guild—should have arrived, and I assure my husband, "Any day someone will come for you."

On the dunghill, I used to welcome the cooling breeze that came in from the southeast every afternoon. In the *caballito*, this breeze feels more like a wind, and it's been whipping up the sea so that water slops over the sides. Since the water disappears into the *caballito's* reeds, there's no need to bail, and neither Roberto nor Alfonso have missed a beat in their rhythmic paddling. Nor have they veered from the course they set on leaving Pisco, not even when enormous sea lions surfaced nearby and swam alongside or, worse, somersaulted, making the *caballito* bounce crazily.

Despite the boatmen's steady paddling, there's still nothing but bleak, inaccessible cliffs on one side, vast, restless ocean on the other. Chufat was not exaggerating when he'd said Peru's coast is desolate! How much further before there's sign of people, paying work?

My back stiffened long ago. My fingers, strangled by

the reeds in which I sank them, are swelling. But I force them deeper. The *caballito* has been narrowly scraping past jagged rocks, slicing through waves so monstrous that Roberto and Alfonso are shouting back and forth.

Can they hear each other, see through these torrents of blinding spray?

Why does it feel like we've taken wing—slammed into inky darkness. . . .

My head an explosion of bird cries and thundering surf, I sense rather than hear Roberto encourage, *"Venga, amigo. Venga aquí."*

Painfully prying my fingers out of the *caballito*, I reach out, feel Roberto grab my arms, hoist me up. My knees snag on something flinty, my feet slip-slide on slime, and as my eyes adjust to the darkness, I realize we're in a cavern, on a rough-edged slab of rock slick with fresh bird droppings.

Once I'm standing steady, Roberto releases me. His moon face vanishes, and I panic. Then I see he's just leaning down to take a bundle from Alfonso, still in the *caballito*.

I want to help. Afraid of slipping and tumbling off the ledge, capsizing the *caballito*, and tossing Alfonso as well as myself into the churning black water, though, I'm too slow. Roberto, moving with his usual confidence, is already setting the bundle on the ledge, turning, and directing an urgent deluge of words at me.

I catch only a word or two, but I think I understand: It isn't safe to go any further for the day; we'll pass the night here.

"*Sí*," I say.

"*Vaya con Dios* ," he responds.

What?

"*Vaya con Dios*," Alfonso bellows from the *caballito*.

The words resound in prolonged echoes.

Vaya, go.

Con, with.

Dios. A name?

Ai, Roberto has vaulted back into the *caballito*, which is catapulting out of the cavern on the crest of an outgoing wave!

As I stare in shock at the narrow arch through which Roberto and Alfonso have disappeared, birds screech; there's the slap of mountainous flesh against rock; I hear horrifying barks. Is the cavern home to sea lions, sea lions that are hauling themselves up to this ledge for an attack?

Shuddering, I back away from the edge. All too soon, rock grazes my ankles. Turning to face the wall, I hunt for a higher outcropping.

I see many.

But they're bristling with birds.

Or too small.

Too drenched by spray.

Too difficult to reach.

I realize then that Roberto and Alfonso did not chance on this particular ledge, and for them to have brought the *caballito* to it so swiftly and unerringly, they must know this cavern well, believe I'll be safe here until Dios comes.

How long will I have to wait for Dios? Can I figure it out from what Roberto and Alfonso left me?

Lest I slip and need to catch myself, I clutch knobs of rock in my sore, puffy fingers while squatting. Once firmly planted on the ledge, I clasp the cloth-wrapped bundle with both hands, lodge it between my knees.

Wah, the knot is secure, and my fingers are clumsy because they're swollen. But I finally work loose two loops of the cloth wrap, revealing the sides of an earthenware jar topped by a metal tin.

The knot completely undone, the entire wrap falls to the ledge, and I recognize the cloth is the kind of blanket-like cloak loaders wear. The tin, easily opened, holds rice boiled with beans. The jar has water.

I have yet to eat or drink today, and my belly, pinched with hunger, rumbles; my parched throat throbs. Bending, I press my lips to the mouth of the jar, seize the earthenware handles, tilt it. Water flows into my mouth, my throat, and I gulp greedily—once, twice, three times before setting down the jar and picking up the tin.

Eating with my fingers, salt stings my myriad nicks and cuts, but the rice and beans, spiced with peppers, are delicious, and when a bird swoops down, loudly demanding a share, I shout, wildly swinging my free arm. The bird is undaunted and the noise attracts more. Dismayed, I quickly replace the tin's lid. Still birds swarm over me, shrieking, squawking, swatting me with their wings. In the fracas, my hat is knocked askew, the water jar teeters dangerously. Screaming even louder than the birds, I throw my arms around the jar. Talons pierce fabric, my back. Pointy beaks stab metal, peck my fingers clutching the tin, the jar. Will persistent stabbing crack the clay? Too anxious to take that chance, I toss the tin into an outgoing wave. Instantly, the birds abandon me to dive after it, and although I know the sacrifice was necessary, I regret its loss.

WAVES DASHING AGAINST rocks and walls wash off much of the waste from sea lions and birds. Even so, the stink in this head-splitting echo chamber is loathsome, and I doubt I need knobs of rock pressing into my back to keep me awake. But I feel as exhausted as if I have dug a full quota of guano, and to ensure I don't inadvertently sink into sleep, roll off the ledge, and drown, I sit leaning against the cavern's rough wall. Wind gusts in with the waves, and my cloak is as damp from spray as my clothes. There's no chance of their drying either, not in this dark, dank hole. Drawing my knees up to my chest, I wrap my arms around my legs for warmth. Still, I'm cold. But I am no longer a captive on the dunghill, and given the rations the boatmen left me, I expect Dios will take me from this cavern tomorrow.

Who is this Dios?

Someone who must be as familiar with these waters, this cavern as the boatmen, and as willing to help me.

Unless I've been fooled by the boatmen as I was by the buyer in Callao, the giant in the Macao pigpen, the man-stealer in the market town.

No.

I can't believe that.

I won't.

And yet. How many stories have I heard from pigs snared by devils posing as benefactors?

But those devils sought out their victims. I approached the boatmen, and they've shown me true friendship.

Then why did they bring me to this cavern?

I don't know. But they must have good reasons, reasons that, when revealed, will win both my approval and gratitude.

~

NIGHTFALL TURNS THE cavern's gloom ink black. Although there's no relief from the relentless crash of waves and spray, the sea lions and birds settle on their rocks and ledges, stop their squabbling and bantering.

Now, in the lulls between waves, I can hear sea lions grunting as they shift positions, even their sob-like breaths, and I'm reminded of night-sounds in the sleeping shed, the diggers I left behind.

Ah Kam would, I'm sure, sneer that I'm no better off here than on the dunghill. Certainly I realize I've a long way to go before I reach home. Without the boatmen's generosity in befriending a stranger, however, I wouldn't have made it this far. And when, with my first earnings, I buy paper, brush, and ink to tell my family I'm free, I swear I'll also write the emperor on behalf of those yet in captivity.

"*You?*" Ah Kam scoffs.

"Yes. I, Wong Yuet Lung, will petition the emperor as Fook Sing Gung once did. I will."

⌒

DAY DRAGS INTO night again. Hard as I've stared at the arched entrance, there's been no Dios, and the backs of my eyes burn like coals; disappointment sharpens my hunger, the stiffness in my arms and legs.

Could I have misjudged the rations?

True, there was barely rice and beans for two meals in the tin. But in this damp, food would sour quickly, so giving me more would have been wasteful.

The jar still has water for several more days. Surely that means there's no cause for alarm. Dios will come tomorrow or the next day or the next.

Unless Roberto and Alfonso, blinded by the cavern's darkness, ran the *caballito* onto a rock and drowned.

Of course, if they'd not returned to Pisco, Miguel and Luis would know. But can they tell Dios where to find me?

The fear that I might be trapped grows. So, too, does awareness of my fault: It was my slowness in climbing from *caballito* to ledge and my failure to help transfer the bundle that prevented Roberto and Alfonso from leaving the cavern as quickly as they should.

Are they now lost to their families?

Am I?

—⁓

THE FAMILY'S PROFIT from the extra generation of worms exceeded our expectations. But the long-awaited letter from the merchant guild turned our joy to ash: My husband was sold to a master who flaunts his cruelty and any attempt to redeem Ah Lung would add to his troubles.

Yet the letter was not without hope. A merchant in the guild has a Peruvian wife with a nephew in the area, a boatman who'd almost certainly agree to rescue Ah Lung were it not for the lack of a common language between the two. "This merchant will send his son to talk to the nephew. Together they may find a way to surmount the language problem."

Anything is possible with help from Heaven. I learned that when I fooled the fortunetelling bird and its master yet failed to make good my plan to outwit my father's greed, and the God of Luck intervened. He brought me to my husband then. Surely he'll intervene again and restore my husband to me.

⁓

BIRDSONG AND THE trumpeting of sea lions herald day-break. Cold to the marrow, my eyes and nose stream; my joints ache; I'm too stiff to rise.

But I have to believe Dios will come, and I will not delay him as I did Roberto and Alfonso. So I force back my shoulders, stretch my spine, my neck, my arms, cracking my joints one by one. Then, grabbing knobs of wall, I heave myself to my knees, my feet, stamp the numbness from my legs.

⁓

I CANNOT COUNT the times I've dropped to the ledge in a painful graze-grasp, graze-grasp of knobs and bumps so I'd be ready to board a boat I'd seen on the crest of an incoming comber—only to discover it had been imagined. This time, however, my name bounces off the rocky walls as I pitch onto my knees.

Ah Lung! Ah Lung! Ah Lung!

Eagerly I peer over the ledge, search the convulsion of water below. And when I see a scow, the bent head and powerful shoulders of a boatman expertly nosing it under the ledge, relief bursts from me in a shout.

"*Gracias*, Dios!"

Gracias Dios! *Gracias* Dios! *Gracias* Dios!

As my thanks echoes, the boatman looks up, grinning.

"Shouldn't you be thanking me?"

The moon face seems like Roberto's, but how could he be speaking in the city dialect?

Questions crowd my lips. Determined not to delay us, I swallow them and turn, then lower myself into the scow as fast as my stiff limbs and raw fingers allow.

"I'm Roberto's cousin, come to take you home."

My heart rocks like the scow under my feet. But Roberto's cousin keeps the boat from upsetting. Indeed, he's already catching a wave, and we're racing into the light, to Bo See.

ACKNOWLEDGMENTS

THE EMOTIONAL SEED for this novel came from my parents, Rita and Robert Drysdale.

For hard facts about the pig trade and Peru's Chincha (Guano) Islands, I consulted depositions from captives, their kidnappers, the captains of devil-ships, and members of their crews; the memorials and correspondence of Chinese, British, and American officials; and articles and books by nineteenth-century abolitionists, journalists, naturalists, and travelers. The footnotes in Arnold J. Meagher's 1975 doctoral dissertation *The Introduction of Chinese Laborers to Latin America: The "Coolie Trade," 1847–1874* directed me to many of these sources. Evelyn Hu-DeHart, a scholar currently working in the field, brought Meagher's dissertation to my attention. She and two other scholars, Lisa Yun and Ricardo René Laremont, kindly sent me copies of their articles, which provided additional information and direction. Philip Choy trusted me with rare books from his personal library. Him Mark Lai, in answering my endless questions, offered necessary context. Discussions with Yvette Huginnie and Jack Kuo-Wei Tchen helped me formulate my ideas.

For my understanding of nineteenth-century life and independent spinsters in Sun Duk, I drew on the work—some unpublished—of Andrea Sankar, Alvin Y. So, Janice E. Stockard, and Marjorie Topley; diverse articles in Chinese from the archives of Him Mark Lai and Judy Yung, translated by Ellen Lai-shan Yeung; Cheung Ching Ping's collection of weeping songs, *Hok Goh Gee Tse*, located by Tsoi Nu Liang and Tsoi Hoi Yat, translated by Ellen Lai-shan Yeung; and interviews with spinsters—Lee Moon, Leung Chat Mui, Tam Ngan Bing, and Yiu Lau Fong—made possible by Tsoi Nu Liang and Hu Jie. Bo See's skills in raising silkworms came from a compilation of seventeenth- and eighteenth-century Chinese treatises on the subject.

I obtained this obscure text and most of my other source material through the efforts of the resourceful and dedicated staff in the San Francisco Public Library's interlibrary loan department, in particular Ron Romano. Lourdes Fortunado, Roberta Greifer, and Carol Small at the Noe Valley branch, Wei Chi Poon in the Asian American Library at the University of California, Berkeley, and Judy Yung also aided my search.

Former POW Eddie Fung shared valuable insights from

his years as a slave laborer in Burma during World War II. He—together with Dorothy Bryant, Deng Ming-Dao, Peter Ginsberg, Robin Grossman, Nan Hohenstein, Marlon Hom, Evelyn Hu-DeHart, Caroline Kraus, Hoi Lee, Miriam Locke, Don McCunn, June McLaughlin, Valerie Matsumoto, Peggy Pascoe, Peter Rothblatt, Tsoi Nuliang, Jan Venolia, Ellen Lai-shan Yeung, and Judy Yung—offered helpful criticism of the manuscript at different stages, sometimes more than once.

Kathy Daneman has long supported my work, and she introduced me to Laura Hruska, whose thoughtful, skillful editing gave the novel its final shape.

Laura Blake Peterson, Peter Ginsberg, and Dave Barbor, my agents at Curtis Brown, Ltd., have provided astute and welcome counsel for much more than this book.

I continue to rely on my husband's analytical eye, passion, and faith.

To all, I extend my heartfelt thanks. You're my luck.